ANY WAY YOU HAUNT IT

ELLEN RIGGS

Free Prequel

Rescuing this sassy dachshund would be a lot easier if he were actually alive.

Novice psychic Janelle Brighton has been framed for murder and a cocky canine ghost holds the key to the mystery. Can they rescue each other before a killer prevails? Join Ellen Riggs' author newsletter to get this FREE prequel to the Mystic Mutts Mysteries series at **Ellenriggs.com/mystic-mutts-opt-in**.

Any Way You Haunt It

Copyright © 2022 Ellen Riggs

All rights reserved. Without limiting the rights under copyright reserved above, no part of this publication may be reproduced, stored in or introduced into a retrieval system, or transmitted, in any form, or by any means without the prior written permission of the author.

This is a work of fiction. Names, characters, places and incidents are either products of the author's imagination or used fictitiously. Any resemblance to actual events, locales, or persons, living or dead, is entirely coincidental.

ISBN 978-1-989303-93-1 eBook
ISBN 978-1-989303-92-4 Book
ISBN 978-1-990613-65-4 AudioBook
ASIN B09KQ3S2MP Kindle
ASIN 1989303927 Paperback

Publisher: Ellen Riggs
www.ellenriggs.com
Cover designer: Lou Harper
Editor: Serena Clarke
2404251537

CHAPTER ONE

Mom cast a critical eye over me and shook her head. "I don't like it, Janelle. I really don't."

I smoothed my hair and dress, wondering what aspect of my appearance had offended her this time. At 32, it would be nice to think I was immune to her judgements but that would take considerable therapy. My current bank balance suggested that wasn't possible.

"Investing in shoes was possible but not your mental health? Priorities." The comment came in a deep, melodious voice. Definitely not Mom's.

I directed a glare toward my shoes, where Mr. Bixby, my tan-and-black dachshund, sat offering judgments of his own. "Never mind," I said. "And stay out of my thoughts."

"Possible," he said. "But unlikely. I like to pop in for a look now and then. Just to see what you're plotting."

Mom joined the dog in a laugh. "Ditto. We have your best interests at heart."

"I'm plotting to open a jewelry and gift store. That's all I have time for right now."

"Priorities," she said, repeating the dog's rebuke. "Bixby and I could help you put them in the right order."

"Just focus on packing, Mom." I gestured to the open suitcase on her canopied bed. "Anyway, what's wrong with what I'm wearing?" I swished the wide skirt of the robin's egg blue dress. "I mean, other than everything?"

The outfit in question belonged to Mom and would be better suited to a Fräulein in an alpine town. I'd sold most of my things before moving back to Wyldwood Springs about a month ago. The rest were still boxed after my grandmother shipped them from the Briar Estates, a gated community that wasn't as safe as the promotional literature touted. For the moment, I continued to borrow clothes from Mom's extensive wardrobe. We both liked to present well but our tastes differed.

"What bothers me is that my clothes look so much better on you," she said. "The past six months turned me into an old lady." Glancing at the oval floor-length mirror, she frowned. "My hair is an absolute fright and I'm down to skin and bones."

It was true that her once-dark hair was a wild tangle of graying curls and her pink dress hung on her. She'd been stuck in a bunker without amenities for some time while a magical crime lord was trying to banish her from Wyldwood. Permanently.

When I found her about three weeks ago, Mom's face was gaunt and lined from a combination of stress and poison. A special tea she drank by the gallon had already made her complexion youthful again but it would take longer to beef her up.

"The salon at the Briars will get your hair sorted in no time," I said. "And Gran will feed you well."

"Your grandmother's strengths don't lie in the kitchen." Turning away, she muttered, "If she has any."

"Mom! That's a terrible thing to say about your own mother."

Her fingers trailed along the edge of the large suitcase. "You say worse about me."

I crossed to an ornate oak armoire, selected a couple of dresses and carried them to the bed. "I would never say something like that. You're the strongest woman I know. When it comes to magic."

She took the two dresses from me and crammed them into the suitcase hangers and all. "You had to add the disclaimer."

"Isn't magic what matters most to you?" I pulled the dresses out, removed the hangers, folded them properly and placed them carefully in the suitcase. Packing was one of my finer skills because I'd moved so many times after leaving home in my teens. "Gran's strength is in loving people."

Grabbing the dresses, Mom cast them aside in a heap. "She doesn't accept me or my style sense. Neither does my sister."

I went back for two more dresses I wouldn't be caught dead in, folded them nicely and added them to the suitcase. "Gran's a beatnik. We all have different tastes and according to some reliable sources, we look pretty good no matter what we wear."

Mom's frown eased. All the Brighton women had attractive features, vivid green eyes, great posture and a sharp wit. These qualities were consistently encoded in our genes in a way magic was not. Mom and I had psychic powers, unlike Gran, my Aunt Eva and my cousin Jilly Blackwood. We'd all felt judged by each other at one point or another, which was a shame when we had so much in common beyond magic.

"A beautiful insight," Mr. Bixby said, using our private internal communication channel. My reception was spotty because I was still getting used to this ability, whereas Mom was an old hand. She had no compunction about listening in on my silent conversations with the dog or regular conversations with friends when she felt like it.

She always felt like it.

"Well, I don't want to see Bridie," she said, distancing herself from her mother by using Gran's first name. "And I don't want to stay at the Briar Estates. It's like a graveyard for the living."

I laughed. "I loved living at the Briars and might have stayed forever if Gran hadn't pushed me out of the graveyard."

"Before you got plowed under." Mom blew out a gusty sigh. "I can't believe you let a hexed woman—"

"Whatever." I refolded a dress and set it on top of the others. "It all worked out."

"Not without aging you." Mom yanked more things out of the suitcase. "You should try my special tea."

I took a pastel peach dress from her hands. "Stop messing with my packing. You'll miss your plane. Or is that the plan?"

Giving the pile of dresses an exasperated shove, she glared at me. "Why are you stuffing so much in? I'll only be gone a week."

Not if I had my way. I wanted her gone longer. Far longer. Ages.

"Gran needs you right now, Mom. You know that. And I spent a lot of time getting the Briars community organized. It'll take someone with your special gifts to protect those seniors."

The glare softened. "And who's going to protect you, Janny? You've got a target on your back."

I lined up the dresses once more. "Me, that's who. Plus Mr. Bixby."

She sniffed. "No offence to your ghost dog familiar, but the Brighton family's enemies could squash him like a bug."

"Offence taken." Mr. Bixby's voice was imperious now. "With all due respect, Shelley, I'm no longer a ghost. And FYI... I don't take crap from anyone but Janelle."

Mom and I both laughed. Mr. Bixby didn't take crap from me, either. Usually he was the one dishing it. Reaching down—way down—I touched his sleek floppy ears. We hadn't known each other long but I loved this dog and his cheeky attitude.

"Understood, and I apologize, Mr. Bixby," Mom said. "I'm just a little frazzled. It would help to know Janelle's been doing her homework. I haven't seen that spell book open since I came home. There's so much I need to share."

I opened dresser drawers and pulled out other essentials. "You always made me do my own homework. Struggling builds independence, you said."

"That was about useless subjects, like math and English. This is different. It's about keeping you alive. You can't just read off a spell and count on it landing properly."

The dog snickered. We'd already seen the proof of her words. Still, I'd rather make a few explosive mistakes than be micromanaged by my mother. And I was less likely to need to use magic at all if she left town. Oscar Knight, the most powerful warlock in Wyldwood Springs, had a hate on for both of us but he'd agreed to leave me alone if I could keep Mom out of his way.

"We'll be fine till you get home," I said. "Once the store is up and running, I promise I'll turn my attention to the rest."

"About this store, Janny—"

"Whimsy?" I cut her off. "You mean my greatest passion other than Mr. Bixby?"

"Whimsy. What a silly name. There's nothing whimsical about Wyldwood."

"Interesting. Mr. Knight said the same thing."

She pressed her lips together, indignant at the mere idea of agreeing with Oscar about anything. "We don't run stores like ordinary people, Janelle. You need to focus on your life's work, not peddling trinkets to tourists."

I grabbed her jewelry box and set it gently among the clothes in the suitcase. There were some valuable pieces in there that would belong to me one day. For now, they were safer in Mom's care. "I'm thrilled about opening my store, Mom. If you can't say anything good about Whimsy, don't say anything at all."

She continued to pull things out of the suitcase as fast as I could put them in. "Fine. I'll come back for your grand opening next week. We'll start our magic lessons then."

I added some pajamas, including a set made of flannel. With any luck, she'd be gone through winter. "Sounds good. Can Sinda and Renata join in?"

Plucking the flannel out of the pile, she threw it over her shoulder. The pants landed on Bixby, who let out a disgruntled yap.

"No, they cannot." She went to collect an armful of shoes from a rack. "Witches only. People like us don't have time for friends or other whimsical things."

"I thought we didn't use that word. Regardless, whatever we are, Ren and Sinda are the same."

She dumped a load of shoes on top of the dresses I'd carefully refolded. "Witch *is* a terrible word, but decades of dodging the label didn't save me from getting poisoned and chased out of town like a stray dog. Nothing against stray dogs, Bixby."

"I wasn't a stray. In fact, I *couldn't* stray from that jewelry store until I was set free." After a moment, he added, "And don't forget the 'mister,' sister. Since you persist in insulting me, I refuse to answer without it."

"As if you'd refuse to speak." Mom tried to force the cover down on the suitcase. "You like hearing your own voice."

He chuckled. "Guilty as charged. I was silenced for decades until Janelle brought me back over to the land of witty conversation."

"You haven't told me exactly how that happened, Janny," she said, as we wrestled with the suitcase. "You've corporealized two ghost dogs now. As far as I know, that's unprecedented for our kind."

I forced the lid up again. "I don't understand it myself. All I know is that it happens at the exact moment I desperately need help. Like a miracle."

She elbowed me away. "Liberating ghost dogs isn't something

I'd brag about. Not when there are people in town who could lift this house from its very foundations and transport it to another dimension. With us in it."

I elbowed her back. "Mom, stop already! Half the shoes you packed aren't paired."

She twirled and flung herself on the bed, face up. "Oh, who cares how I look?"

"You! You care. Appearances are half the battle, like you've always taught me."

She rubbed her face, careful to avoid smudging her makeup. "I should have taught you something more practical. I failed as a mother."

"Not completely," I said. Mr. Bixby poked my shin, in a not-so-subtle reminder to be nice. Being nice was more likely to get Mom on the road. "I'm here, aren't I? Helping you pack?"

"I mean I failed as a *witch* mother."

That word was like fingernails on a chalkboard, but debating would only prolong our farewells. Ten years in the hospitality industry had given me the skills to resist her bait.

"Again, I'm still here, aren't I? I survived on the run for years, outwitted a couple of murderers, and even got Oscar Knight to back down." Tucking matching shoes into the right spots helped me keep my cool. Organizing what I could kept me from worrying too much about what I couldn't. "I'm going to be just fine until you get back."

She propped herself up and glared again. "Don't think I didn't notice you packing for permanence. There's no way I'm leaving my home and Sir Nigel unprotected for more than a week."

The man in question appeared in the doorway. Sir Nigel Boswell hadn't actually been a man for more than a century. He was our family ghost—a loyal and devoted butler—who managed to pass for human due to a charmed talisman. "You called, madam?"

"I didn't," Mom said. "Not yet."

Zipping the suitcase closed, I smiled at him. "I did, Boz. Mom's ready to go."

"Oh, thank goodness," he said. "I was afraid we'd miss the plane."

Mom moved to the edge of the bed. "*We?* You're not coming with me, Sir Nigel."

"Of course I am, Miss Shelley. My place is at your side. Always."

"Unless it's at Janelle's side." She shoved herself upright. "Her need is greater than mine at present."

Boz lifted the large suitcase as if it were as light as the air he essentially was and started walking. It had been easy to find his forged documents and book him a seat on the plane. He was still in his typical morning suit, however, which would look mighty odd in more tropical climes. That was Mom's problem, now.

"After failing you for months, I refuse to let you down again, Miss Shelley," Boz said. "Let us go. I brought your car around to the door."

"He drives?" Mr. Bixby sounded outraged. There was no love lost between Sir Nigel and my dog, but they were beginning to understand and possibly even respect each other. Boz had pledged to protect Mom just as Bixby had me. It took a village to keep the Brightons alive.

"Yes, he drives," Mom said, still refusing to leave the bedroom. "That's part of his role."

Mr. Bixby let out a disgruntled snort. He very much wanted to drive but while he had exceeded the abilities of any dog, being in a dachshund's body came with certain limitations.

We herded Mom after the ghost, correcting course several times before we got her through the spacious front hall and outside. I grabbed my purse and locked the door.

Meanwhile, Boz held the rear passenger door open. I guided

Mom in for a safe landing and even buckled her seatbelt, while he circled the car and got behind the wheel.

"Give Gran a hug for me, please," I told her.

"I will not. We Brightons have no use for such nonsense. It leaves your back exposed."

I tried to give her stiff body a squeeze. "Mr. Bixby has my back, which leaves me free to splash hugs around."

After closing the door, she rolled down the window and stared at me. "Do not touch that spell book, Janelle. *Everyday Spells for Everyday Magic*. Honestly. The title's as whimsical as Whimsy."

I shrugged. "It came with that name. Anyway, you just said you wanted me to practice magic."

"Under strict supervision. Mine, specifically. At this point, you're a hazard. You blew the door off your store and caused extensive plumbing issues here. Spectacular backfires."

"Hit it, Boz," I called, tapping the car. The ghost butler did just that, flooring it out of the driveway. His heavy foot surprised me, especially because he had initially learned to drive a horse and carriage.

"Show-off," Mr. Bixby said. "Bet Sir Windbag gets pulled over."

Perhaps Mom chastised the butler, because he faded from sight for a moment and made it look like she was a passenger in a driverless car. By the time they turned the corner, however, he was back to offer a jaunty wave.

Mr. Bixby and I released twin sighs of relief.

"I was starting to doubt I could pull that off," I said.

"Never doubt yourself, Janelle. You are one heck of a packer." The dog trotted over to my car and then gave me a fetching head tilt. "Now, how about letting me drive this old heap?"

CHAPTER TWO

Elsa, my bronze sedan, was old but she was most certainly not a heap. I had treated this car like a priceless gem since I got her when I was barely 17. As a result, she did her absolute best to get me out of some difficult situations as I crisscrossed the country working in high-end hotels and resorts. Most recently, she had nearly flamed out while trying to save Mr. Bixby and me from magical miscreants as we came home to Wyldwood Springs.

"It's a car," the dog said, from the passenger seat. "She isn't sentient, unlike yours truly."

"You don't know that for sure," I said, taking the long route into town. I needed to cross some of the many pretty bridges and creeks to ease the stress of shipping Mom off. My anger at her for not standing behind me when I was a teen had mostly passed, thanks to a more mature understanding of the politics at play in town. But sharing a roof with her, as well as a ghost butler and a former ghost dog, hadn't exactly been easy. I'd spent as many waking hours at my new store as I could. "Maybe Elsa will surprise me like you did and become another best friend."

"Doubtful. If there was a spark in the rust you'd have known it long before now."

"I can tell you one thing, Mr. Bixby... If Elsa were alive, she'd have a nicer tone than yours."

He turned one of his gorgeous brown eyes on me. "Nice doesn't keep you sharp and alive. Wit and wisdom do that. Those I have in spades. Not to mention good looks."

"Don't forget ego. There's no shortage of that."

He blinked. Or winked. I could only see one eye. "As a height-challenged dog, and then a prematurely deceased one, I worked hard to bolster my confidence. While stuck waiting for you, I studied personal development."

"Personal development? How?"

The "duh" in that brown eye was obvious. "Google. These boots aren't made for walking but they can work a keyboard."

I ran my fingers over his shiny coat. "I'm lucky to have such an evolved companion."

"*Familiar*. Just say it."

"I won't. That's tantamount to admitting I'm the other word. The one we banned from our lexicons along with wiener, remember?"

"And sausage." He tapped the handle to direct me to wind down the passenger window. "But denial can only take us so far. Many do call me a wiener dog and you a witch."

"As far as labels go, I prefer 'friend.' It's a word to celebrate today with Sinda and Renata. But before that, let's give Gran a call. I promised to update her about Mom's mood so she can self-medicate accordingly."

He stuck his nose out the open window and pulled in gusts of the effervescent Wyldwood air. It smelled like cedar, moss and wildflowers, and danced like champagne on my tongue. I enjoyed it so much I almost didn't mind what it was doing to my hair. Why hadn't I covered my curls with a scarf?

"Because silver screen siren isn't your look," Bixby said, snickering.

"It used to be my look. Or one of them, anyway. Before I took to the alps in Mom's wardrobe."

A bit of his spittle flew back and hit me in the cheek. "You made a decision to fly under the radar in nerd-wear so stop chafing about it. Resistance is futile."

"Star Trek now? I thought you were a Star Wars fan."

"I was a fan of anything that would distract me from my life before living again." He looked at me over his shoulder, and I felt the smile that his doggie lips couldn't quite form. "All in the rear view, thanks to you."

"Don't give me all the credit. You made the decision to cross back and join Elsa and me in a life of danger and delight."

At least I thought it was a combined effort. My knowledge of magic was sketchy at best, and that was deliberate. What I didn't know or care to learn couldn't hurt me, I'd always figured.

Until that wasn't true anymore.

Now I had to take it more seriously. Develop my dubious skills. I could read minds with varying degrees of proficiency. I could pick up impressions and memories from stones and other natural objects. And when pressed, I could deliver a little shock, like a human taser.

"Not so little," Bixby said. "Three people are sitting in the slammer with scrambled neurons, thanks to you. I wish you'd left them enough capacity to remember how despicable they are."

"One day I might be able to calibrate more carefully. For now it's shoot first and let them ask questions later. At least they can't overshare with the police."

"Or one specific officer." Bixby chuckled. "You only care about Big Red's opinion."

That's what he called Chief Andrew Gillock, a clever, handsome man I'd briefly considered dating when we met in Strathmore County near Gran's gated community. Drew had asked some pointed questions about my actions when someone died down south, however. When someone died in Wyldwood, he followed me here to ask a few more. Our tiny bud of a romance had frozen in time because I couldn't answer those questions. Wouldn't if I could, as it would put him—and perhaps many others—in danger.

"That's not true, Bixby," I said, pressing Gran's number on my phone. "But if Drew's sticking around to help the local police, I need to watch my step."

He continued to chuckle even after Gran picked up at the other end. She knew about Bixby's abilities but she could only hear his articulations as growls, yaps and mumbles. That made my life easier. I needed to put her fears to rest and he'd only exacerbate them.

"Janny!" Her voice filled my heart with warmth and sunlight. I pictured her in her typical peasant skirt, jingling bangles and daisy-studded sandals, although she'd been going through a prepper phase lately, thanks to my cousin's eccentric friend, Edna Evans. "How are you, sweetheart?"

"Couldn't be better, Gran. Mom's on her way, special delivery."

The pause at the other end told me Gran was nervous about the visit. She loved her daughter but was a little scared of her, too. Most people were scared of Mom, including me.

"Not me," Bixby said. "With people like Shelley, you just need to come on strong. Tell Bridie that."

"It'll be fine, Gran. Mom's mellowed a tad. You just need to come on strong with her."

"That was Mr. Bixby's idea, wasn't it?" Gran said. "I heard his mumble. Does he know your mother?"

Bixby and I both laughed. "Yep, and he practices what he preaches. He put Mom in her place a few minutes ago and she took a telling."

"Shelley won't take a telling from me. A helpless human who needs protection from her daughter and granddaughter."

I ran my index finger along the cracked vinyl of the steering wheel. This situation required a delicate touch. "Gran, Mom's nervous, too, believe it or not. She knows you've got all the people skills she lacks and she feels she's let you down. Just like I feel I let her down by having people skills and too little magic. We've got some interesting family dynamics but when push comes to shove—"

"Which it always does," Mr. Bixby interjected.

"We all love each other," I finished. "Right?"

"Right," Gran said, without much conviction. "I'm glad you and your mother are getting along better and I'm sorry to pull her away even for a short visit when you need her."

"Actually, I need her gone, Gran. There's a situation in Wyldwood, and the longer you can keep her at the Briars, the better."

"I can't fool your mother, sweetheart, and if there's no situation here, she won't stay. What happened was an accident."

"Tripping off a curb is an accident," Mr. Bixby said. "Getting blown into traffic by a strong wind is not."

"I know what he's saying," Gran said. "His tone is a giveaway."

"Don't think he doesn't enjoy hearing that. But he is right. You got blown in front of a tour bus by a sudden, powerful wind that affected no one else."

"It was fine. No one was hurt."

"The driver got banged up when the bus blew over, according to Chief Gillock. No one can explain what happened."

"How is Drew?" she asked, eager for a diversion. "Are you two making some headway?"

"Gran, romance isn't on my radar right now. I just want to launch my store and enjoy some time with Sinda and Ren."

"It does my heart good to hear you say that. I know this magical business requires attention but it's important to prioritize your personal life, too."

"Exactly. I'm trying to be a human instead of a you-know-what."

Gran laughed. "We don't use that word. I don't approve of it and neither did my own mother, who could rightly claim the title."

My great-grandmother apparently had a heaping helping of the Brighton magical genes.

"You know what, Gran? I wish we could either all get the genes or all skip the genes. It's caused friction between Mom and aunt Eva, and between Jilly and me."

"I got along fine with my sister, Elaine, but Cousin Liberty... Well, she was a special case."

Mr. Bixby turned from the window so quickly he almost stumbled. Sometimes he was clumsy. Others, he moved with the grace of a weasel.

"I'll let that insulting comparison pass unchallenged," he said. "Only because I want to hear about this special case."

"Mr. Bixby wants to hear about your cousin, Gran," I said, turning off the back roads and heading toward town. "I know you don't like talking about her, but the more he knows about our family and this town, the better he can help me avoid land mines."

"Exactly. It's not just prurient curiosity," he said.

"It's also prurient curiosity," I said.

"Prurient?" Gran laughed. "Well, I don't mind indulging your dog's curiosity if it helps keep you safe." She paused, perhaps gathering the mental and emotional fragments of her cousin's story. "Let me start by saying I loved Liberty very much. Adored her, really, because she was two years older than me and so much fun. I was closer to her than I was to Elaine."

"But then...?" Bixby prompted.

"But then Liberty's magic came in early. Far too early for her to get a handle on it, or for our mothers to train her properly. By second grade, Libby was getting sent home from school for minor infractions that stemmed from immaturity. The nasty little boy who got stuck to the toilet seat, for example. The mean girl who fell into every mud puddle. No one could prove it was Libby, but her mom pulled her out and homeschooled her. That meant Liberty never developed social skills. Eventually she became quite eccentric. Her idiosyncrasies led to her being a pariah in a town of so many pariahs."

"So, she left? Like I did?"

"Around the time you were born, yes. For years, postcards and collectible teaspoons arrived in the mail. And then they just stopped. Eventually we heard rumors that her body had washed up on a beach in Jamaica. By the time we arrived to collect Liberty, it had disappeared."

Mr. Bixby's head tipped to one side. "And you left it at that?"

Gran could hear the question, if not the precise words. "My mother and Libby's did all they could to get to the bottom of it but never found so much as a whiff of sulphur."

The dog pounded the cracked leather seats with chunky paws. "That's a crock."

"Oh, I know," Gran said. "Whatever he's saying, I agree fully. It was bad enough that I lost my cousin, but my aunt was never the same again, either. She also passed away too young."

"So tragic," I said, slowing in the traffic on Main Street. The town was picture perfect, with quaint storefronts covered in trailing vines and planters filled with seasonally appropriate blooms. "Makes me wonder if the Brightons were hexed or cursed at some point."

"I've wondered the same," she said. "I can hear the street noise so you must be close to Whimsy. That name is just perfect, Janny. I'm terribly sorry I can't be there for the opening. I know how much it means to you."

"Too much," Bixby said. "Someone's projecting all her desires for a normal life onto one old haunted store."

"It's not haunted anymore," I told Bixby.

"It's not?" Gran said. "You didn't mention you managed to banish the legendary ghost at Mabel's Fables."

That was the store's original name, but the sign that said "Whimsy" was now in place. I could see it from down the street—

white scrawling script standing out over fresh red paint. There were as many flowers adorning the storefront as I could manage, and I was constantly adding more. Winter would steal them all from me soon, but they'd last through the launch.

"Banish is the wrong word, Gran. Bijou is a poodle-cross who was bound to the store until I—"

"Made a big mistake and pulled her over," Bixby said. "A more annoying creature never lived."

"Brought her back," I finished, ignoring him. "She lives with Renata now and they couldn't be happier."

"Now *that* is a wonderful gift," Gran said. "Bringing ghost dogs back and finding their perfect home. I am so proud of you."

A lump formed in my throat. "Mom thinks it's a useless gift."

"Quite the opposite. You wouldn't be where you are now if not for Mr. Bixby."

"You got that right, Bridie," he said. "They don't make dames like you anymore."

I repeated the last part for Gran, knowing it would delight her.

"Dames," she said. "I like that. Makes me feel special."

I slowed and found a parking spot right in front of Whimsy. That spot was nearly always vacant and I liked to see it as a sign that the universe wanted me close.

"Gran, you are special. You're the most important person in my life, with a little competition from Mr. Bixby, who isn't a person."

"Who isn't *just* a person," he corrected, "but so much more."

"Thank you, sweetheart. I'll do everything I can to keep your mother at the Briars, short of getting blown under another bus." She paused for a second. "The thing I can't figure out is how it missed me. A tour bus."

I reversed into the parking spot and turned off the car. "Easy. A bigger wind."

"Coming from where?"

"Either from someone who didn't want you squished or from

someone who wanted Mom to come down there to investigate. Those are my best guesses."

"Oh. Well, that's interesting." I sensed her circuits were overloading but she knew how to compensate. "Janny, I'm so glad you have this time to spend with friends and enjoying everything you missed. But please tell me you'll also put some energy into learning magic. This bus business is worrisome."

"Mom will figure it out. Nothing to worry about, Gran."

I stared at the wide store window and realized there was very likely something to worry about on my end, however. The window seat that Bijou had recently vacated was occupied today by another canine of the spectral variety.

Bixby didn't bother with words, howling his outrage in more typical dog language.

"Oh my, what's upset dear Mr. Bixby?" Gran asked.

"Another dog," I said. "Looks like an Australian shepherd."

"I've always liked a herding dog." Gran had to shout over the barking. "So smart and efficient."

I hoped so. I really did. Because every time I met a ghost dog it seemed to mean chaos.

CHAPTER THREE

"That's my turf," Bixby said, scratching at the car door. "Release me immediately to evict the trespasser."

"Mr. Bixby, we're not leaving this car until you calm down. If we have another canine guest, we'll extend our hospitality for as long as it stays."

"That ghost doesn't belong here. It was Bijou's store and then it was empty. Ghosts are tied to one place."

He was too worked up to think logically. It didn't happen often, so I gave him a moment to collect himself before saying, "We just sent a ghost onto an airplane with Mom. Sometimes they do get around."

His paws came down with a little thud. "Oh, right. Sir Windbag has a talisman. Are you saying this canine interloper has one, too?"

"No idea. But there's a ghost in the store who wasn't there yesterday and I would imagine it's come for a reason. How about we go in and find out?"

His agitation eased as I opened the car door and then carried him to the store. "I can walk, in case you've forgotten."

"I know. You're bred to forge into dark tunnels and kill badgers. But the way I see it is that every new dog, living or otherwise, should be regarded with a dose of caution. You're precious to me, Bixby."

He grunted as I shifted him to the other arm to unlock the door. "Not precious enough for you to remember the 'mister.' And I would like to meet a potential adversary on my feet."

"How about we hear the dog out? For all we know, he may be here to help us, just like Bijou. If not for her, we wouldn't own this place."

"Well, now we're set for life. Another dog we don't need. Two's a crowd, three's a pack—and packs get noticed."

"True, but we're very much on Oscar Knight's radar, anyway." I twisted the key in the lock. "He sends his henchman around daily to remind us he's watching. Maybe this new dog has valuable intel."

"He doesn't. Look at those eyes. Vacant. Stupid."

I left the key in the door and stepped back to survey the visitor through the window. "There's nothing stupid about a herding dog. You think highly of Keats, don't you?"

Keats was a brave and brilliant border collie who belonged to Jilly's best friend, Ivy Galloway. Together, they'd put plenty of deadbeats behind bars. Our new guest undoubtedly had some of the same qualities.

"I think highly of myself. No other dog has my particular skill set. Can Keats become invisible? No, he cannot."

"Don't even think about fading," I said, finally cracking open the door. "I need to see you to protect you. We're a team, remember?"

The little bell over the door normally gave a jolly tinkle as I came in, but today it sounded a wary note. I was getting used to its moods but this was new.

"Stay where you are," I told the Australian shepherd. "Just for a moment, please."

The Aussie wasn't taking requests. Instead, the ghost hopped off the window seat and dropped to a herding crouch. Mr. Bixby's temper triggered and he writhed until I set him down. Sometimes you just had to let dogs be dogs. How much trouble could they do on different planes of existence?

My dachshund dashed at the Aussie and they both launched at the same moment to collide mid-air. Of course, Bixby passed right through the ghost and gave a convulsive shudder as he landed.

"Like an Arctic gale," he said, staggering slightly. "Now I know how Bridie felt when that bus blew over."

The Aussie returned to the window seat with a bound and sat prettily, mouth hanging open in what seemed like a cheery pant. To passersby, he was completely invisible, whereas to me, he was a gorgeous tricolor dog that probably once weighed about 60 pounds and might again by the time we were done.

"Welcome to Whimsy," I said. "Appearances to the contrary, we're happy to have you here."

"Maybe *she's* happy," Bixby said, jerking his muzzle in my direction. "I am not."

"We'll end up fast friends soon enough, I'm sure." I walked over to the window seat and offered my fingertips for the dog's inspection. He took a cursory sniff that was more for old time's sake—a time when his nose still worked. "What can I do for you, sir?"

Bixby glared at me. "Sir? What's with the formalities when you can't even spit out a mister?"

"Feels right on first acquaintance." I thought about kneeling to face the new dog but that hadn't worked out well in the past. The town's gossips were always spying and it would look like I was either praying or uttering incantations. No need to throw logs on the rumor fire that burned plenty bright without my help. Instead, I sat carefully on the seat beside the dog and waited for his next move. When he lifted one white paw, I turned my hand palm up and the ghost rested his paw on my hand. There was no weight to it, but I felt a distinct tingle. A connection. The sensation confirmed there was a spark of life in this currently lifeless creature. "I'll do my best, sir."

"Oh, for pity's sake, you're not bringing this one back, too." Bixby paced under the window seat. "Bijou didn't have the decency to go far. How many revived ghosts do you need around here?"

"As many as the universe sees fit to send. According to Sinda, this is my true calling."

"You have too many callings to handle as it is. Jack of all trades, master of none."

I turned away from the Aussie and glared at my dachshund. "Who's dishing crapola now, Bixby? I've only been a jack of this particular trade for a month and managed to liberate two dogs."

"Accidentally."

"The first was an accident. Namely, you. The second was deliberate. I may not know the exact mechanics but I assume they can be learned."

"Your mother said this dubious ability is unprecedented, which means there's no rule book for ghost dog rescuers."

A little sigh escaped me as I stared at the Aussie. It sure would be nice to have a beginner's manual to speed things along. "I guess I'll need to figure it out as I go."

Mr. Bixby looked from the ghost to me and back. "Well, what does he want?"

I turned the question more kindly to the Aussie and got silence as an answer.

"See?" Bixby said. "Stupid."

"On the contrary. This is an intelligent dog who's decided not to talk. I'll need to earn his trust, just as I did Bijou's. In the meantime, maybe Sinda can help."

No sooner did I say my friend's name than I heard her footsteps on the basement stairs. We both loved being here and she was often in her studio working on jewelry designs long before I arrived and after I left. When Mom came back, Sinda had moved from the manor to a local bed and breakfast to give us family time. I appreciated the gesture, but for the moment I was happier hanging with friends. Mom and I would need time and space to get used to each other again.

Meanwhile, Sinda and I worked together seamlessly getting Whimsy set up. She split her time between designing and helping me learn the ropes of running a store. Though well into her seventies, she had plenty of energy—and more than she'd had when I met her down south. In Strathmore County, she'd been retired by force from her own jewelry store by an ambitious niece. Solving the murder of said niece had brought us together, freed Mr. Bixby, and started a beautiful friendship. I hoped she'd stay forever.

"Good morning, you two," she said, smiling. Her gray curls were a bit longer and softer now and flattered her face. There were fewer lines around her eyes and mouth, and I wondered if Mom's special tea had worked some magic. Ren and Sinda had initially been slow to recover from being poisoned and Mom had insisted they partake of her special herbal blend regularly and often. Taking a closer look at us, Sinda's blue eyes widened behind the glasses she only needed now for jewelry design. "I mean, good morning you *three*. Apparently, a newcomer arrived after I went downstairs."

When Mr. Bixby lived in Sinda's store down south, she'd never been able to see him, although she caught his likeness in a pretty pendant with an emerald chip for an eye. I touched the pendant now and it gave off a comforting warmth. It was my talisman.

"This is Harold," I said, finding the dog's name had arrived in my mind at the right moment. "Harry to his friends."

"He's hairy all right," Mr. Bixby said. "This one is going to shed like the dickens when he joins us in primetime."

Sinda came over and offered the dog her fingers. His backside gave a little wiggle but there was no tail to wag. I would have to rely on other cues to read his mood.

"So, he's come to find you," she said. "Word of your skills must be spreading, my friend."

Bixby collapsed dramatically in a sunbeam on the hardwood floor. "Don't say that, Sinda. We'll never have a moment's peace."

She bent over to give Bixby a pat. "I had years of peace, as did you. Boredom, in fact. We chose differently for our next act, did we not?"

"Should have read the fine print," Bixby said, rolling so she could give his other side equal attention. "I didn't know it would be a revolving door of canines in need."

I loved how easily Sinda adjusted to whatever fate threw at us. "Is there an Australian shepherd in your special collection of pet jewelry?" I asked.

Straightening, she pulled her phone out of her smock pocket and swept her finger across the screen a few times. "Aha! Believe it or not, that was the third piece I created. Right after my flying dachshund and the prancing poodle. Perhaps they're arriving in order."

The dachshund in question lifted his head. "Exactly how many of these so-called jewels are there?"

Sinda gave him an enigmatic smile and dropped the phone back into her pocket. "I like to keep busy and so do you, old friend."

In her former jewelry store, I'd seen at least a dozen little dogs on display. Hopefully fate would space them out more so that I could learn the ropes. It wasn't like I just snapped my fingers and welcomed them to the land of the living. There had been a fair bit of excitement in the lead-up and real drama in the actual crossover.

Now wasn't a good time for drama and sending Mom south was part of the plan to reduce it. The store's renovation was complete, but the shelves were still mostly empty. Aside from Sinda's wares, it had been hard to source the type of products I wanted. I wouldn't carry anything that didn't fit with my vision of Whimsy, so if we had to start sparsely, that was okay with me. Over time I'd discover exactly what I was meant to offer. It should all unfold naturally and eventually this little strip of three stores would be a thriving hub that attracted a steady stream of the right customers. We'd build our community one person at a time.

"Community," Bixby muttered. "Sounds cumbersome. Stay light and lean in case we need to run. Again."

"No one's running anymore," I said. "We stand and fight for what we have."

Sinda smiled around our expanding circle. "Community sounds just about right. I love being surrounded."

A thud from next door made us all turn and stare at the wall between Renata's space and mine.

"Let's give Harold some time to adjust," I said, moving swiftly to the door, "and go check on our neighbor."

CHAPTER FOUR

Any loud thump made me nervous these days but when we walked through the unlocked door of Ren's store, my childhood friend was behind her brand new counter looking healthy and happy. Her dark eyes were lined elaborately and dramatic red lipstick made her white teeth look even brighter as they framed a sheepish smile.

"Sorry about the noise," she said, twisting her long dark hair into a messy bun. "Norm says the espresso machine is fighting back."

A white head appeared over the counter and nodded to us. Norman Jenkins represented a high-end distributor and happened to live nearby.

"Morning, ladies," he said. "This is the finest machine money can buy, but it puts a load on the grid. I'm taking extra precautions."

"As a co-owner of the building, I appreciate that," I said, stooping to pick up Mr. Bixby. Ren's space in the short strip of three attached stores needed significant renovations and there were hazards all over. In fact, Ren usually crated Bijou in the back to keep her safe. It had previously been run as a bistro by Ethan Bogart, who'd moved down the Main Street strip to expand. "And as a coffee fan, I'm eager to try your wares."

"Gimme five," Norm said, disappearing again. "Nearly done."

Renata came around the counter, beaming now. This place was a long-held dream come true. She'd initially planned to run a simple bakery but I'd given her the espresso machine as a "store-warming" gift. I wanted her to think bigger from the get-go. She'd been forced to live a small life working in someone else's café and there was plenty of business for two in Wyldwood Springs. Besides, as a coffee devotee, I loved the idea of popping next door several times a day to sip with my oldest friend. It was the icing on the cake of our reconnecting after a long rift.

"Are you sure you can't open next week with Whimsy?" I asked, staring around. "It's nearly done, right?"

Ren shook her head. "Far from it. It's been hard finding help in town. After what happened."

She was being deliberately vague because of Norm. Unlike many contractors and services, he'd crossed the unofficial line to help Ren because he knew her from her long stint working at the Beanstalk Café down the street. Oscar Knight had sold us the building and kept quiet about his reasons, but that hadn't stopped the rumor mill. The tenant in the flower shop on the other side of Whimsy had terminated her lease suddenly, leaving the space vacant, and we'd both had to bring in help from other towns to get set up. Ren's major remodeling was challenging.

"Such a shame, when you two will be contributing so much to the community," Sinda said. "It's petty."

Ren's smile didn't dim a bit. "I'm happy to take my time and savor every minute of the work. I never thought my dream of running my own place could come true. If it takes longer, who cares?"

Norm's head popped up again. His warm brown eyes had a distinct twinkle. "Who ya got for beans, Ren? What I brought will only last two days if your friend here guzzles like you said."

Ren's face flushed. "I never said guzzles."

I laughed. "I own it. Whereas you and Sinda guzzle Mom's tea, I prefer coffee. So, like the man says, who ya got for beans?"

She held up crossed fingers. "Diggory Waring from Rare Earth is coming by this morning. His company sells the best organic, fair-trade beans and it would be a total score if he'd agree to supply me."

That should be a given but Oscar Knight was blackballing us at every turn. As the owner of more than half the real estate in town, he could afford to make our failure his mission. Losing this building to me in a strange twist had hit his pride hard.

Norm got to his feet and his bristly white moustache lifted to reveal a proud smile. "Showtime, ladies. Who wants to pull the first shot?"

"You do the honors," Ren told him. She was wary of coffee machines and this one looked capable of taking a spaceship into orbit.

As Norm worked his magic, Mr. Bixby squirmed in my arms and gave a loud snort. He'd been quiet because of Norm but holding in his witticisms usually came at a price. I was likely to be hit with a barrage of them shortly.

"Do you smell something?" he said, lifting his muzzle.

"Coffee," I said. "I smell coffee. The best smell in the world."

"Guess again." His nose rose even higher. "Release the poodle."

Ren turned and handed me a small white cup filled with steaming black brew, eyebrows rising in a question. I nodded a response. If Mr. Bixby actually wanted a second opinion from Bijou, I wouldn't stand in the way.

"What's going on?" Norm said, as Ren headed into the back room. "I feel like I'm missing something."

"Ren just misses her dog," I said. "They're still on their rescue honeymoon."

Mr. Bixby's next snort was derisive, but his body stiffened. Bijou, the fluffy apricot formerly-deceased poodle cross, bounded out of the back room with her usual energy. Then she stopped and stiffened, too.

"Uh-oh," she said. "Stinky stinky stink-bomb."

"I hate to agree with her," Bixby said, "and I really mean that. But two noses are better than one when it comes to detecting magical flatulence."

Sinda, Ren and I exchanged glances. That term was Mr. Bixby's inimitable way of describing bad magic. He claimed it smelled like a mixture of rotten eggs, fermented lawn waste, and roadkill. This heady bouquet appeared to be beyond detection by the human nose, or even a trio of late blooming—"

"Witches," Bijou supplied, in her quirky, chirpy voice. "One, two, three. Never enough for me."

Before we could figure out what to do next, the door opened and another trio of women came in. Mr. Bixby gave an exaggerated retching sound to dispel any doubt in my mind about their intentions. It was a little disappointing as I had hopes of winning over the locals.

Mitzy Lennox, the silver-haired woman in front, was someone I'd known all my life. She owned the Beanstalk Café, of which I had very fond memories. Gran took me there often when I was a child. When I returned to Wyldwood, however, Mitzy made it clear the fondness only cut one way and her frown today confirmed it.

Behind her stood two equally dour middle-aged women. One was Becca Mathews, who ran a rather upscale pet boutique named Small Wonders. The other was Matilda Wentwhistle, a hair stylist at A Cut Above, one of two salons in town. The latter was single-handedly to blame for my mom's current curl problem. Matilda either didn't know how to handle a mane like my mother's, or she deliberately mismanaged what should be a fine head of hair. I made a mental note to take my own locks out of town when I needed a trim. My long-held belief was that great hair made for a great day.

"Piffle," Mr. Bixby said, causing Sinda to smile. Luckily the new women couldn't hear him, despite someone giving off unpleasant whiffs that suggested magical capabilities.

I was about to speak when Renata came forward, with Bijou doing little semi-circles from behind, like a herding dog. It was Ren's storefront, after all, and I had to defer to her. Further, as a Wyldwood lifer, Ren knew these women far better than I did.

"Mitzy, it's so good of you to come." Ren sounded both nervous and proud. I knew her former boss hadn't always been kind but she had offered a consistent pay cheque when Ren was on the wrong side of the town's rumor mill. "Welcome to my as-yet-nameless bakery."

Sharp blue eyes pinned my friend through rimless glasses and Mitzy shook back her polished bob. "Just call it doomed, Renata. Your startup is dead on the launch pad."

Ren flinched and stepped back, while Bijou offered a series of sharp yaps and said, "Mean-mean-meanie."

The poodle's warning bounced off Mitzy, so I spoke in Ren's defense. "Why so harsh, Mitzy? You know Ren's been training to run a bakery for a decade. She earned certifications and worked at half a dozen places before taking this leap. It's far from doomed."

"It most certainly is doomed because it's not just a bakery. After all I've done for you, Renata, you had to stab me right in the back by opening a café. You're stealing the bread from my table. Starving my children."

Mitzy's two kids were older than Ren and me and had left town years ago.

"There's plenty of room in the Wyldwood market for more cafés, bakeries and bistros," I said. "Our population is growing by leaps and bounds."

Matilda Wentwhistle stepped forward from the ranks of the Main Street posse, and I admired her carefully highlighted layers. She'd done a good job on her own hair, it seemed, as well as many other women in town. I could only assume what she did to Mom was a deliberate styling assault. "Why couldn't you just offer bread, Renata?" she asked. "Coffee puts you in direct competition with your generous mentor. As for you, Norman Jenkins, I'm shocked to see you here."

Mitzy glared at the old man before spitting out, "Traitor. I had the only machine like that in town. How can Ren even afford it?"

"A payment plan, no doubt," Matilda said. "It probably costs more than my mortgage."

Norm wasn't in the least flustered. If anything, his twinkle game intensified. "Ladies, this machine is paid in full. How about I pull you a shot and we let bygones be bygones? All's fair in love and business."

Ren straightened and squared her shoulders. She was naturally shy and had tried to fly under the radar most of her life, but like me, she was determined to turn over a new leaf now. "Mitzy, I'm sorry you see things this way. Baking will be the main event here, but if someone wants to grab a coffee on the way out, I figure it only makes sense. You offer so much more at the Beanstalk than I ever could, with my limited space. Most of your business comes from brunch and even light dinners. That's out of scope for me."

Mitzy crossed her arms. "So you say now. If you'll steal my coffee business, I'm sure you'll stop at nothing. But I can tell you one thing, Renata Scott: you will never get my beans."

"Your beans?" I asked.

She turned her fierce gaze on me. "Everyone knows I offer the best coffee in hill country, Janelle. You said so yourself when you got back, and then went ahead and made an end run on me. But Renata can't plow me under without my beans and I'll make sure Rare Earth knows she's a very bad risk."

The door opened and a balding man stepped in. His receding hairline seemed to give more real estate to nice eyes and a very pleasant smile. Looking around the circle, he said, "Did I come at a bad time?"

"You sure did, buddy," Mr. Bixby said. "Unless you want a ring-side seat at the cage match."

"Break it up, break it up, bite 'em fast," Bijou said. She was always high energy but Ren's agitation had pushed the frenetic dog over the top. "Do something, wiener boy. Walk the big talk."

My dog struggled to get down and I obliged. I didn't see how he could possibly help, but something had to give.

Mitzy's scowl told me this was Diggory Waring, purveyor of fine coffee beans.

"Hey, Diggs," Renata said. "We should probably talk later."

"Better yet, not at all," Mitzy said. "Your services won't be needed here, Diggory. But I do need to speak to you immediately at the Beanstalk."

Diggory looked confused. "What's going on?"

Bixby strutted around the room. "He's not the brightest bean in the bag, is he?"

Sinda pressed her lips together but Ren was too worried over the tension to appreciate Mr. Bixby's humor.

"Step it up, small stuff," Bijou said. "All brag, no bite."

He glared at her. "This is your domain, is it not? But if you insist, well, I suppose I'll contain the situation for you. Never let it be said I'm not a team player."

"Bixby, leave it," I said, through our internal channel. "Let this run its course."

Instead, my cheeky dachshund took a run at Ren's window seat. In all the hubbub, I'd failed to notice that Harold, the Australian shepherd, had joined us. I didn't expect him to be able to pass from place to place so easily. He was a ghost dog with a little extra, it seemed.

"Over to you, Hairball," Bixby said, yapping up at the sheepdog. "Earn your keep."

Harold cocked his head and then crouched. With one leap, he

crossed the store and landed behind Diggory Waring and the three women.

Although they couldn't see him, apparently they *felt* him because they all moved forward in lockstep.

Harold circled so fast he became a tricolor blur to me and an invisible tornado to them. A trio of high-pitched squeaks and one in a lower register suggested all of our guests knew they were being air-herded out of the store.

As last in, Diggory Waring was first out, and he didn't hold the door for the ladies. Matilda and Becca followed at a run, letting the door swing back in Mitzy's face.

"What on earth?" she said, silver hair blowing around in a cloud. "Have you rigged up a wind machine, Renata?"

"Industrial fan out back," Ren said. "To help with fumes."

Mr. Bixby gave a showy retch to suggest nothing could dispel magical flatulence, even the tumult caused by a ghostly sheepdog.

"This isn't over," Mitzy called as she yanked open the door. She lurched out as Harold hit her square in the buttocks. "Not by far, Renata."

"Oh, it's over," Mr. Bixby called after her. "Don't let the door hit you on the way out."

The door did hit Mitzy, though, and Bijou laughed. "Score. Score. Score. One point for the underdog."

I glanced over at Harold, now back on the window seat and growling in so low a tone maybe only I could hear it.

This ghost was no underdog. He was more powerful than any canine specter I'd encountered. Harold was a working dog on a mission... and I had a feeling I'd be doing most of the work.

CHAPTER FIVE

"What just happened?" Norm Jenkins said, rubbing his hair hard enough to send white strands flying in the last of the breeze. "It was like they saw a ghost."

"People are so easily spooked around here," I said. "Seems like they freaked out over a fan."

His eyes continued to twinkle and I marveled over Norm's equanimity. "Tempest in a coffee pot," he said. "If it doesn't work out with Rare Earth, I can get you some decent beans, Renata. Diggs Waring isn't the only game in town."

"I could never go with Rare Earth now," Ren said, pacing. "Mitzy's started a campaign against me. There's no point throwing gas on the fire."

Norm turned and pulled another espresso, filling the store with a heavenly fragrance. "Don't bite off your nose to spite your face, though. Mitzy's all bark."

"Bite bite bite," Bijou said, leaning against Ren's legs. "Shoulda woulda coulda."

Mr. Bixby glared at Bijou. "And yet you deferred to me."

"And you deferred to Hairball," Bijou said. "Big talker short walker."

This time all of us smiled, including Ren. Norm had his back to us, so it seemed safe enough to enjoy the moment.

"I'm sure this will simmer down long before you open," I told Ren. "Mitzy's just hurt you moved on. You worked hard for her and now it's your time to shine."

"Agreed," Sinda said, taking the next espresso from Norm with a grateful smile. "You can never hold someone back from their calling, and she's always known running a bakery is yours."

"I still feel bad," Ren said, declining a coffee. "Although I hated working for Mitzy, to be honest. No matter how early I came in, how late I stayed or what new recipes I tried, it was never enough. I didn't take vacation for four years, yet she gave me a hard time for going to my favorite customer's funeral."

"Time to run your own show," Norm said. "Have a coffee and let's toast to your success."

"Norm, I can't," Ren said. "My stomach's in knots. I could never handle much discord. That's why I stayed at the Beanstalk too long. I was afraid to leave."

"Tell you what," the old man said. "Let me go down there and smooth things over. Maybe Mitzy's burned because she's got an old clunker of a refurbished machine. I could give her a deal on a good one."

"Aw, Norm, thanks," Ren said. "I tried to get her to switch years ago. It's a crime to waste the best beans on that old thing. You've kept it alive long past its time."

"It's a moody beast," he said. "With what she's spent on repairs Mitzy could have had two of these babies by now." He gave the new machine a fond pat before gathering his gear. Then he said his goodbyes.

We all heaved sighs of relief as he left. As sweet as Norm was, dealing discreetly with this trio of special dogs wasn't easy. Now we could all be ourselves, including Harold, who was pacing restlessly on the window seat.

"Who's the new boy? Or girl?" Renata said, brightening. Another dog was clearly a happy addition as far as she was concerned. Like Sinda, she was able to see this ghost, whereas she hadn't seen Bijou till the poodle crossed. It was more evidence their powers were growing quickly, despite my mother's disparaging comments.

"Hairy hairball," Bijou said. "No one invited him."

"For once I agree with you, Miss Talk-a-lot," Bixby said. "I won't make a habit of it."

I wagged my finger at them. "You're jealous, both of you. Harold is most welcome in our building and look how he's just helped us."

"Nothing in life is free," Bixby said. "What does he want in return?"

Harold jumped off the bench and started rounding us up. The wind was indeed palpable and my curls blew into my face. Ren's hair tie slipped out and her long hair lashed, while Sinda pressed hers down with both hands. Meanwhile, both dogs got forced back against a ladder that rattled and clanged. I stooped to pick up Mr. Bixby, while Ren did the same with Bijou.

"Easy, Harold, easy," I said. "Seems like you want us to move to Whimsy, but please don't hurt our dogs. No matter how rude they are."

Mr. Bixby struggled in my arms, enraged. "I'll show that herding fool what I'm made of. I've got moves you can't see."

"Don't you dare go invisible," I said. "He will too, and then where will we be?"

Harold dialed back the wind power and we walked to the door. "How about we knock a hole in the wall in the back to come and go?" I said, watching the Aussie pass through effortlessly.

"Good idea," Sinda said. "I have the feeling we're all being watched."

Once we were in my store, I set Bixby down and closed the

blinds. Harold was nowhere to be seen, so I felt we could proceed with my original plan. Namely, Magic 101.

"Your mom told you not to do that," Bixby said, strutting after me.

"Gran said the opposite, didn't she?"

"Do what?" Ren asked, pouring tea from the thermos Mom had sent along with me.

I went into the back room and returned with my spell book. "This. Mom gave me a hard time for not practicing and then told me not to do it while she was gone."

"She's just worried, I'm sure," Sinda said. "I am, too. It takes so little for a spell to go sideways."

"We did well the last time," I said. "And I've had a few other successes. We'll never get better if we don't try."

Mr. Bixby made a huffing sound. "Why couldn't you try when Shelley was here to serve as a lifejacket on the stormy seas of magic? You've gone overboard a couple of times."

"I can't relax with Mom backseat driving. She's so intense and we're more easygoing. Everyone has a different magical style."

"Is that so?" A sweep of his nose constituted a request to be put on the counter. "Well, I look forward to seeing your easygoing style, then."

I lifted him but stopped with his paws dangling. "Maybe you'd be better watching from below. Just in case."

"Aha! All this easygoing blather is a front." He kicked his short legs. "I insist on being close at hand to give you confidence."

Sighing, I set him on the counter. Despite his crusty bluster, this dog did give me confidence. It wasn't in his words or delivery but the sheer fact of his presence in my life. We had made powerful magic together when he crossed back over. Unprecedented magic, according to Mom. Then it happened again with Bijou. I had the goods, I just needed to work on the delivery, and that was what today was about.

Renata caught my eye and tried to smile. "I'm not too nervous because I doubt I can pull off a spell, yet. Especially not today. My nerves are jangling after that run-in with the Main Street posse."

"Relax, Ren," I said. "We're going to start small. Very small. There's no downside to this spell, from what I can tell."

Bixby paraded across the counter, nails clicking on the polished oak. "You checked the encyclopedia of unintended magical consequences?"

"That would be so handy," I said, bending to collect what we needed from the shelf below. "Remind me to visit the library to check out some reference materials."

I placed three small plastic flowerpots on the counter, each containing a small seedling. Ren and Sinda faced me on the other side, and it was nice to see them both brighten.

"Oooh, this looks like fun," Ren said. "Now I'm up for it."

Bijou went to her old perch on the window seat, checked for Harold, and then jumped on. "You can do it, Rennie," the dog said. "Do it up big."

Bixby turned to stare down at her. "Your unrelenting positivity serves no one, poodle."

Renata laughed and ran her hand over him. "It serves me perfectly, Mr. Bixby. Some of us need that."

I looked from one dog to the other. "No distractions, please. We need our full focus, even for Magic 101."

Ren chose one of the pots. "How does this work?"

"It's a simple growing spell," I said. "No special ingredients required."

Sinda leaned over to look at the open book. "Love it. What are we growing?"

"That part's a surprise," I said. "Even to me. They were in unmarked brown bags at the convenience store."

"Somewhere down south your mom is cringing," Bixby said. "Unmarked could mean poisonous."

"Why always so negative, wiener boy?" Bijou called, crossing her paws. "When you could bring out the best best best."

He let his short legs give out in a dramatic protest and I decided to ignore both of them. My biggest challenge with magic was focus. I wasn't quite sure how to get in the right state of mind and it was one question I had asked Mom. She'd looked at me as if a zombie had stolen my brain and said, "You just *do*. It's innate."

And that's when I decided to do my own homework.

"So, here's what I'm thinking," I said. "We just hold onto our little pots and say the spell. Try to picture the plant growing and give it some sunshine and energy through our fingertips. How does that sound?"

"Worth a try," Sinda said. "I'll go first." She leaned over to read the short spell and then clasped her hands around her little pot. Closing her eyes, she spoke the words: "*Only I know what may grow when I sow the seeds of power.*"

My eyes fixed on the plant but I heard the rise and fall of Sinda's even breaths. She was so confident, calm and composed that it didn't surprise me one bit when the seedling sat up and took notice. Its two little leaves suddenly became four and then six. Meanwhile the stalk shot up about a foot. A bud appeared and then opened, as if it were time-lapse photography. And there it was: a perfect pink gerbera daisy.

"Well done, Sinda! Well done." I grinned as she opened her eyes.

The flower got bigger, threatening to tip the small pot, so she released it. "Oh my, how lovely. Gerberas are a favorite. My mother always grew them."

"Fantastic," I said. "That's the biggest gerbera bloom I've ever seen."

"Not too showy?" Sinda asked, laughing.

"Just enough. It shows assurance. Flair. Like the designer you are."

"My turn, my turn," Ren said, eagerly.

"Add one more repetition and you and your dog will become twins," Bixby said. "I wanted more for you, Renata."

"She got what she needs," Bijou said. "Me-me-me."

Glancing at the spell, Renata followed Sinda's example, lacing her fingers around the pot and then speaking the words aloud.

Nothing happened.

Eyes still closed, Ren murmured, "I can't feel anything. What am I supposed to feel, Sinda?"

Our friend rested her fingers on Ren's arm. "I imagined space around me. Sunlight. Warmth. The smell of the springs. That felt like the right climate for growth."

Ren's perfectly groomed black eyebrows gathered and I sensed she was trying too hard. Still, the seedling started to grow. It straightened, stretched an inch, and sprouted another pair of leaves.

When her dark eyes opened suddenly, however, the seedling drooped till its leaves hit the soil.

I applauded anyway. "You did it, Ren. You made that thing grow."

She blinked a few times. "But then it just... died."

"It's not dead, it's resting," I said. "Still green and waiting for more love. Can you describe what you were thinking?"

Closing her eyes, Ren pondered. "At first, I did just as Sinda said. Imagined myself at Withrow Park standing in the mist by the falls. But then the Main Street Posse arrived in my head with Diggory Waring. And I noticed colors around them. After that, I couldn't focus."

I rested my elbows on the counter. "Colors? Like an aura?"

Ren's pretty face scrunched. "I guess. I've never seen auras before, but there was color today. Yellow for Matilda. Orange for Becca. Blue for Diggs Waring. And very dark for Mitzy."

"Very dark?" Mr. Bixby said. "As in black?"

She opened her eyes. "Smokey gray, maybe. I think I was having a panic attack and lost my focus."

Touching her arm, I asked, "Do we have auras? Sinda and I?"

Staring at us, she nodded. "Sinda's is sort of metallic blue. And you have a rainbowy haze around you, like the full color spectrum." After a moment, she added, "It sounds silly."

"On the contrary, it sounds cool," I said. "Maybe this is one of your special powers, Ren. Let's check it out on the street later. In the meantime, I'm going to see what I can do with this plant."

I clutched my little pot, excitement filling my chest and putting another smile on my face. Could I grow a flashy sunflower, for example? Fill the store with its cheery bloom? The ceilings were high enough for it.

A familiar energy flowed into my fingertips and I focused on sunshine and effervescent air. There was indeed a smell of moss and damp vegetation and a strange whooshing sound. I continued to picture the sunflower but the pot seemed to change and rock in my hands, and it was hard to hold it steady.

"Janelle," Mr. Bixby said. "Too much of a good thing is actually a bad thing."

"Stop, Janny," Ren said. "It's crazy."

The sunshine and sweet scent of growth vanished suddenly from my mind, replaced by clouds and a whiff of something distinctly sulphurous. The tingling in my fingertips turned to heat and I let go of the pot with a gasp, opening my eyes.

Sinda and Ren both screamed and I instantly saw why. My plastic pot had exploded with roots and a fat stalk rose to the ceiling. The head of a large, heavy sunflower had slumped over and was now turning from yellow to black. Smoke filled the air and the store's fire alarm let out a shriek.

I was trying to figure out what to do when the whole plant collapsed in a heap of ash. It blew around in a dust cloud that made us all cough. Mr. Bixby hacked a few times and then stuck his muzzle under Sinda's arm, which no doubt felt like safer haven than mine at the moment.

After a few minutes, the dust settled over all of us leaving Ren's black hair with a gray cast. "What just happened?" I asked.

Sinda pulled an embroidered handkerchief from her smock pocket and patted her eyes and lips before sneezing. "Dear friend, I've seen nothing like it before. You grew a spectacular sunflower so suddenly it threatened to drill through the roof. Then, just as suddenly, it started smoking. And you saw the rest."

Mr. Bixby pulled his head out and shook from head to tail, sending ash flying. Then he did it again and again, just to make a statement before his official statement. "You tell *us* what just happened."

Leaning over, I shook out my hair and then dusted myself off, as best I could. "One minute I felt like I was in a huge greenhouse and I could literally see my sunflower shooting up."

"But then...?" he prompted.

I caught the dog's eye and sighed. "Magical flatulence. It filled the greenhouse and I wanted to save my flower. It felt like I was holding on too tight and I guess I detonated the poor thing."

"And mine," Ren said, pointing to her little pot, where the seedling was no longer just resting.

Even Sinda's gerbera had experienced an untimely demise.

"I feel terrible," I said. "These poor things were alive and I killed them."

Mr. Bixby shook again, somehow finding a little more ash to send into the air. "It's not all on you, I suspect. Check out your new guest."

Bijou had vacated the window seat in favor of Harold, the Australian shepherd, who seemed to have swelled to twice his former size with raised ghostly hackles. He stuck his nose through a crack in the blinds and let out a chilling growl.

"I bet I know what happened," I said, walking around the counter.

When I cracked the blinds, I expected to see Oscar Knight standing outside. Instead, it was the heavily gelled man I called Officer Slick. Sometimes he wore a uniform with a small neon insignia, and I assumed he was a member of the magical police force. Other times he seemed to be working off the books as Oscar's personal security guard. Regardless, he visited often and at random, no doubt to keep us guessing.

Normally his presence caused some internal recoiling, but I wouldn't have thought it sufficient to turn a towering sunflower to ash. Maybe there was more to this guy than met the eye. Or maybe Oscar Knight himself was adding some foul air to my neighborhood.

Turning back to the others, I said, "It's possible someone hijacked my spell."

Mr. Bixby motioned to be lifted down. "Such a shame when a simple spell grows so horribly wrong. Never let it be said that—"

"I know. You warned me of the perils of cockiness, Bixby," I interrupted, setting him on the hardwood.

"Miss Brighton." He used the formal title to underscore the importance of his point. "I illustrate the perils of cockiness daily. How do you think I ended up a ghost in the first place?"

CHAPTER SIX

I hurried down the street after Renata and Bijou, with Mr. Bixby under my arm. "Honestly, Ren, I think you should leave well enough alone."

Glancing back at me, she slowed down. "But it's not well enough. I think Mitzy hexed us. Her aura was as gray as ash."

We both brushed away dust as we walked, probably sending up a little cloud. For the first time I was glad to be wearing Mom's blue dress. You couldn't really see the film covering it and my jacket helped tamp it down. Ren's dark sweater was conspicuously lighter than it had been earlier.

"You should see your hair," Mr. Bixby said. "Bet you wish you were blonde right now. Like Jilly."

"You should see your fur right now," I countered. "Bet you wish you were apricot right now. Like Bijou."

My dog shuddered. "I am a pedigreed dachshund and never have a moment's regret about that, despite some personal challenges."

"Gran would say we're perfect just as we are. Wayward spells notwithstanding. Mom, not so much."

Ren shook her hair loose but the ash barely lifted. "It was my fault," she said, slowing down for us. "I should have realized Mitzy would be burned by my opening the bakery. Guess I got carried away in my excitement."

We fell into step together. "Like I said earlier, there's plenty of business to go around in this town, from cafés to gift stores. People leave town to shop because the options in Wyldwood are scarce. I blame it on Oscar Knight, who manages local real estate like a fiefdom. But the mayor must be backing him, too."

"I suppose, but I didn't want to ruffle feathers. Now there's a new Main Street posse united in hating me."

We walked more slowly, and I sensed eyes on us. Most of them were probably unfriendly but the vibe felt less menacing today. "I guess it was inevitable that a new posse would spring up and fill the void left by the one we disbanded."

A few weeks ago we'd sent one middle-aged mean girl to prison and two others to sulk in their respective corners. Nature didn't like a vacuum, apparently.

"Matilda and Becca were always nice to me," Ren said. "I don't understand how you can go from being everyone's favorite baker to an outcast so quickly." Her eyes landed on me apologetically. "Scrap that. I *do* understand how attitudes shift in this town. But I'd love to smooth things over with Mitzy before it gets worse."

"How?" I asked. "You can't scale back on your dream to accommodate hers. What are you going to do? Launch a different business?"

"I can start by returning the espresso machine. That's the biggest bone of contention, second to the coffee beans themselves. Then Mitzy and I can negotiate a menu that doesn't rival hers."

Mr. Bixby picked up the baton. "Don't you dare make yourself small for the likes of Mitzy Lennox, Renata. You'll deprive the world of java and joy... and for what?"

Bijou stood on her back legs and pirouetted as best she could while confined by a leash. "Right, right, right. The wiener hit the bullseye."

He lifted his lip at her to show a little teeth. "Four on the floor, circus clown."

"No bickering, you two," I said. "Remember we need to use our inside voices in public, and especially when we get to the Beanstalk."

Unlike Ren, I could hear both dogs in my head and switched channels more seamlessly by the day. Hopefully it would become fully automatic before long. I was still frequently caught chitchatting aloud to Bixby and was earning a reputation as being more eccentric than my mother. That took some doing, as she had been carted to the police station a few times for trespassing. She was only searching for ingredients to reverse poisoning, but her nonsensical explanations left people thinking she was addled.

Outside the Beanstalk Café, Ren had no choice but to stop and regroup. The lights were off, the closed sign turned and the door locked.

"How strange," Ren said. "Lunch is peak time." She pressed the buzzer beside the door and then rapped hard on the glass. "Did I upset Mitzy so much she can't work?"

"Call her. Maybe she had an appointment."

"A doctor's appointment," Ren muttered, pulling her phone from her purse and pressing the number. "Maybe I gave her a heart attack."

"Or maybe you're overstating your importance," Bixby said. "Cockiness is contagious, you know."

She gave him a glare for the first time. "Cut me some slack, will you?"

"Careful, Ren," I said. "The rest of the posse is probably spying."

I scanned the street, but that earlier sense of being watched had faded. In fact, the street was strangely quiet for this time of day. A few people ambled along like they hadn't a care in the world. Two women stopped to sniff chrysanthemums in a display outside A Cut Above, but there was no sign of Matilda in the window.

"Call went to voicemail," Ren said, lowering her phone. "Surprised Mitzy hasn't blocked me yet."

"Let's go back to Whimsy and keep trying. We can all put our heads together and come up with a good plan."

Instead, Ren pulled keys out of her purse. "I've got a plan."

"A bad one," Bixby said. "Poodle, she's your responsibility."

"Mitzy never asked me to return the key," Ren said. "That's practically permission to use it."

"Not really," Bixby said. "Bet Big Red would still call it trespassing. Wouldn't you agree, poodle?"

Ren stuck the key in the lock. "I heard Mitzy's phone ring in there. Didn't you?"

Bijou stayed conspicuously silent, although her anxious pacing showed she wasn't in favor of going inside. Her desire to support Ren currently outweighed her caution.

"I heard it," I said. "That doesn't mean she's in trouble."

"But she could be, so the police will understand that I had to go in to help."

Mr. Bixby grabbed Ren's sleeve in his teeth but she was already slipping through the door with Bijou, leaving me no choice but to follow.

"There's always a choice," he said, after Ren shook her sleeve loose. "I smell sulphur in there. Don't you?"

"All I smell is smoke," I said, as we walked through the café. "Must have singed my nasal passages with the sunflower incident."

"Inside voice," he reminded me, on our internal channel. "I smell coffee. And something burning."

"Burning," Bijou said, out loud. "Smokey smoke smoke."

"You're right. Something is burning," Ren said, picking up

speed as she circled the long counter. "There's a fire extinguisher in the— Oh."

She stopped suddenly and we caught up. Ahead of us, someone was lying near the cash register surrounded by coffee grounds and fragments of white china.

"At the risk of stating the obvious," Bixby said, in my head, "something's extinguished Mitzy Lennox."

CHAPTER SEVEN

I didn't believe him, at first. Staring down at Mitzy, it seemed like she was just resting after a tumble. Her blue eyes were open, but they were no longer sharp—would never be sharp again, I realized. About six feet away, her rimless glasses lay crumpled, as if flung aside. Or blown off.

I shuddered at the thought and Mr. Bixby said, "Not a heart attack."

"What then?" I asked, using our internal channel that no one could hear.

He sniffed several times. "Electrocution, I believe. I've had occasion to smell it before." Sighing heavily, he added, "I smelled so many unpleasant things in what was too short a life. We don't use the word 'short,' of course."

"Banished." I gave the dog a squeeze, glad to have a dachshund shield against this distressing situation. "Can you tell how?"

He sniffed again, more delicately. "Not with any certainty, but proximity suggests the espresso machine. Ren said it was old and prone to malfunction."

"But you said you smelled sulphur. What if Oscar—"

"Fried Mitzy's circuits?" he interjected. "Possible. But it's possible she released sulphur when she passed. That happens with the wrong kind of person."

Ren jerked suddenly and started moving. Bijou was tugging her toward the door to the kitchen, which was between us and Mitzy's body.

"Someone left a burner on," Ren said, her feet moving faster and faster. Bijou might only weigh 30 pounds but she'd returned to life with more strength and agility than she'd probably left it.

After Ren disappeared, Bixby cleared his throat. "Janelle, about those earrings..."

I touched my ear. "What about them?"

"Not yours. Mitzy's. Amethyst, I believe. Dime a dozen, but you might get a hit off them."

"Yes, of course. Good call."

He waited a beat for me to move and then added, "Now would be ideal. It's going to get very crowded here soon."

I adjusted his position under my left arm and then stooped to touch Mitzy's earring with my right index finger. A flood of impressions swept through my mind with such power that I dropped to one knee.

One thing was clear: Mitzy had been utterly terrified when she passed. Yet what happened hadn't come as a complete shock.

"No pun intended." Although Mr. Bixby's voice was inside my head, it sounded far away. "Sorry, I can't help myself."

"Not funny," I said, continuing to touch Mitzy's earring and watch the flashes of her memories flick through my mind. There were a few scattered images from her life at home, but most scenes featured the Beanstalk Café. It had been her passion and she had achieved a lot. "I always loved this place and so did Mitzy."

"Time to let go," the dog said, as my grip on him slackened. "Of the earring that is. These paws don't touch cadavers."

I tried to pull my hand away from Mitzy's earring but letting go wasn't easy. My finger felt connected and I was eager to learn more about her life. Finally four sharp pinpricks made a point.

Releasing my wrist, the dog admonished me. "Doesn't pay to stay too long. Especially after someone's passed."

"But I saw—"

"I know what you saw because I *saw* what you saw. Now get up and see how Ren is doing. That poodle's yapping is grating on my nerves."

"Ren," I called. "Are you okay?"

Poking my head into the kitchen, I saw my friend moving pots off the stove with one hand while holding back Bijou. The poodle strained on her leash to get to the back door, barking ferociously.

Mr. Bixby lent his voice to the situation and the noise became deafening.

I eased past Renata and found the door to the alley ajar. Using my elbow to open it more, I poked my head into the alley and saw a woman with a teased blonde bouffant hightailing it around dumpsters and other trash on white sneakers.

"What am I missing?" Ren asked, joining me.

"Ronna Tweeze. Moving like a sheepdog on an agility course."

Ren stuck her head out just in time. "Ronna's been Mitzy's waitress for decades. Maybe she saw something."

"Maybe she *did* something," Mr. Bixby said.

"To Mitzy?" Ren asked. "I doubt that. Her death must be accidental."

"Must it?" Mr. Bixby said. "Normally you'd be the first to suggest questioning everything in Wyldwood Springs."

Ren caught my eye. "Do you think someone killed Mitzy?"

I shrugged. "Inconclusive. But we'd better call the police."

Pulling out my phone, I pressed the number. Before I could spit out more than hello, however, we heard sirens.

"Big Red to the rescue," Bixby said, chuckling.

"Quiet. Please, Bixby. This doesn't look good for us right now."

"Us?" Ren asked. "Why?"

Bijou was an anxious jitterbug on the end of her leash. "Wrong place, wrong time," the dog said.

My dachshund chuckled at that. "Exactly. I look forward to seeing how you handle this one, Janelle. Good thing you've got all those people skills. Time to dust them off. Literally."

"We didn't do anything except come in to help," Ren said.

"Like Bijou says, we're in the wrong place at the wrong time," I said. "I'm sure Drew will understand. Eventually."

Ren followed closely as I walked out of the kitchen and into the seating area of the café. Here we didn't need to see Mitzy, at least. She was hidden by the counter.

"What are we going to do?" Ren asked.

I took a deep breath and patted my hair. "Not sure yet. But follow my lead."

"And she'll follow mine," Bixby said, chuckling again.

"This isn't funny, Bixby," Ren said. "Mitzy Lennox was like a mother to me."

He lifted himself in my arms to get a better look into Ren's eyes. "A very poor one with a smoky aura. Don't go getting sentimental just because she passed."

"Well, I worked with her for years. And Ronna worked with her far longer."

The police gathered on the sidewalk outside. They hadn't noticed us yet, it seemed. "Did they get along?" I asked. "Ronna and Mitzy?"

Emotions battled on Ren's face but she finally shook her head. "Not really. Or not anymore. Mitzy's been so irritable in the past couple of years. I'm not the only one she bullied."

"Still, killing Mitzy at noon in her own café would be a very bold move."

Ren shook her head. "I doubt Ronna could pull that off. She wasn't the brightest knife in the cutlery drawer."

"Let's just put our suspicions aside for the moment and tell the police what we know," I said.

"Always the best policy," Mr. Bixby agreed. "Especially when one's handsome paramour is staring at you with more shock than fondness."

"Drew isn't my paramour." There was a note of sadness in my voice as I realized that prospect had likely slipped even more out of reach. Sometimes I allowed myself to imagine living a blissful normal life with Drew Gillock, but I knew I was fooling myself. We could never have a normal life because I wasn't normal.

"Just relax," Bixby said. "No need to crack my ribs. If you can handle Oscar Knight, you can most certainly handle Big Red. It's not the first time."

That was before I let my guard down ever so slightly with Drew. He had suspicions about me, understandably, given the three murders that had transpired since we met down south. Those suspicions had motivated him to stay here in Wyldwood and help the local police force. His curiosity about me went a little deeper, I knew, but even the most openminded man would be challenged to accept the Brighton legacy.

"True," Mr. Bixby said. "I warned you not to let romance run away with you, didn't I?"

"Hard to keep track of all your warnings. Anyway, quiet on all fronts, Bixby. I need to keep my wits about me."

He gave a huffy sigh. "Fine. You seem to have forgotten how useful I am in such situations."

I pinched the internal conversation line closed as the door opened. The dog's words built up behind the block, so I bit my lip as an additional safeguard against his witticisms. He liked to make me laugh at the wrong time and a crime scene was most definitely that. Now was the time for the smooth-talking hospitality and PR expert to shine.

"Miss Brighton and Miss Scott," Drew said. "What a surprise to see you here." He raised his voice over the blare of the ambulance and fire truck. "We had a call that someone was incapacitated."

"Yes, unfortunately," I said. "Although you arrived just as I called."

"Ronna Tweeze must have called first," Renata said.

James Barrow, a young blonde officer with pale eyes, switched on the overhead lights. Then he came up to stand beside Drew and crossed his arms. "Ronna? Why would you say that, Miss Scott?"

"Because we saw her running out of the alley, Jimmy," Ren said. Once upon a time, she had been Jimmy Barrow's babysitter, and his posture now seemed to dispel much of her shock and confusion. "Ronna left the back door open and my dog was barking like crazy."

Bijou was the soul of propriety now, leaning against Ren's leg to offer the full force of her support.

"Why were you even in the kitchen?" Jimmy asked. "Before calling us to the scene."

"All the burners were on, that's why," Ren said. "I turned them off and moved the pots. When we came in we smelled smoke and I did something about it. I'm a chef by training, as you know, Jimmy."

Drew scanned us continually with his serious eyes. He was impossibly gorgeous, even by my impossibly high standards. I'd done my best to avoid serious romantic entanglements for more than a decade and it helped to keep the bar high for looks, personality and character. Unfortunately, Chief Gillock had been inordinately blessed. I'd never met someone who ticked all the boxes, some of them several times over. "Is that why you're both a little dusty?" he asked. "Was there a fire?"

I brushed my dress again and then shook my head to loosen some ash. "No, but it was close. Ren got to the stove in time. I was behind the counter checking on the status of Mrs. Lennox. I'm sorry to say she was beyond incapacitated when we arrived. Nothing could be done for her."

"What makes you an expert?" Jimmy Barrow asked, directing his pale eyes at me.

"Advanced training in first aid, Officer Barrow," I said. "Starting from my first job as a lifeguard. Every year I renew my certification. You just never know when you might need to help someone."

Jimmy and Drew walked around the counter and stood over Mitzy. They glanced at each other and then Drew held up his palm to stop the rest of the crew from surging through the door.

"You always seem to arrive a bit too late to help people, ma'am," Jimmy said. "Loretta Billings was beyond incapacitated, too, as I recall."

"It was a shame about Loretta and now it's a shame about Mitzy," I said, meeting Jimmy's eyes squarely. The young man didn't drop his gaze as easily as he had before. "I wish we'd come a bit sooner."

Drew kept his eyes on me, no doubt to pick up any nuance of expression. "Why did you come at all? Miss Scott doesn't work here anymore, as I recall."

Ren started to speak, but Bijou quickly silenced her with a mumble that sounded like, "Leave it to Witchy." The dog clearly needed a refresher on the words we'd banished from our lexicon.

"Chief Gillock," I said, "you're well aware that Renata is opening a bakery next to my store. As it turns out, Mitzy Lennox was incensed about that. She came over this morning with some friends to discuss the matter."

"We heard about the fight already," Jimmy said. "I was directing traffic down the road when Matilda told me Ren got all hot under the collar about the coffee maker."

"I didn't lose my temper, but Mitzy lost hers," Ren said. "She was worried my business would steal her clients. And she said I would never get her beans."

Drew's coppery eyebrows soared. "Her beans?"

"Coffee beans," I said. "The secret to good coffee is a combination of the right machine and superior beans. When a Rare Earth rep visited Ren today, Mitzy lost her cool. I suppose she felt betrayed because Ren had worked here for so long."

"No wonder," Jimmy said. "You were stealing the bread right off her table, Miss Scott."

Ren's cheeks flushed and then her dark head drooped like my sunflower had earlier. Bijou let out a growl that caused Jimmy's eyes to widen.

"James," Drew said. "None of us should be speculating about what happened."

"It's not speculation," Jimmy said. "It's exactly what Matilda said."

"Which doesn't make it true," I said. "There were other witnesses, and I assume you'll talk to all of them to get the full picture. By then, you'll realize Ren did nothing wrong."

"Yet she came over here afterward?" Drew said. His eyebrows were casting too much doubt for my liking. "Why is that?"

"Because Renata's a kind person, which you already know. She had a good run with Mitzy but it was time for a fresh start."

"Including a high-end espresso machine," Drew said.

"Correct. And for that matter, the machine was a gift from me. So, I suppose Mitzy should have been mad at me rather than Ren for potentially diverting clients."

"Well, there's no competition now, is there?" Jimmy jerked his head toward Mitzy's body. "The vacancy sign just went up."

Renata gave me a bewildered look. "Is Jimmy suggesting I had something to do with this?"

"He sure is," Bijou said, although thankfully only I could hear her. "Bad Jimmy. Bad bad Jimmy."

"Of course not," I told Ren. "Officer Barrow is reacting impulsively to some gossip. Chiefs Gillock and Dredger will discover in due course that we simply came over to smooth the waters with Mitzy and found her electrocuted."

"Uh-oh." The melodious voice got past the block in my head. "Oversharing, Miss Brighton."

"Electrocuted?" Drew asked, looking down at Mitzy. "What made you come to that conclusion, Miss Brighton? I see no exposed wires. The cash register couldn't deliver a charge like that."

"Just a guess." My voice was a little higher now. Squeaky, even. Mr. Bixby couldn't help chuckling. "I saw something like that once before."

"When you were a lifeguard?" Drew pressed.

"Exactly. And when I ran a marina and tour boat service."

The inner canine grumble got stronger. "Zip it, lady. Zip now or regret later."

"You sure have had a lot of jobs for a relatively young woman," Officer Barrow said.

"Relatively!" My voice went up another notch. "I'm still young, Jimmy."

Renata finally smiled. "We're both old to Jimmy. Remember, I was his favorite babysitter. A fact that doesn't seem to have earned me the benefit of the doubt."

"Being an old acquaintance doesn't get you off the hook when someone is dead," Officer Barrow said. "Someone who happened to be your competitor."

I expected Bijou or Bixby to jump to Ren's defense, but another dog beat them to it. My eye caught a movement near the window. Harold, the ghost sheepdog, was sitting on a high stool, muzzle turning this way and that as he followed the conversation like a tennis match.

Now he crouched for takeoff and then crossed the seating area in a single leap. He landed on the counter in front of James Barrow. The officer took a step backward into Drew and they both staggered a little. Jimmy's wispy fair hair blew back and even Drew's perfect auburn locks lifted.

"Do you feel that?" Officer Barrow said. "It's a cold wind."

Drew looked over at the door, perhaps expecting to find it wide open. It wasn't. The first responders were waiting outside for direction.

Harold jumped down on the far side of the counter, and while I couldn't see him, I suspected from the officers' movements he was herding them toward the body.

"Yeah," Bixby said inside my head. "Do your job, cops."

I covered my mouth to hide a smile as Harold came back over the counter and herded the rest of us up.

"It sure is breezy," I said, as the ghost dog pressed us toward the door. Ash from our hair and garments swirled in the air as he stirred up our personal tornado. "Chief, we need to get going. I'm expecting a service call at Whimsy."

Drew looked nearly as dazed as Jimmy, who had disappeared under the counter, presumably to examine Mitzy. "I need to interview both of you. Formally."

"Of course," I said. "You know where to find us."

"I'll find you at the old manor," he said, reeling back as Harold ran around the counter for another blow. "Go home."

Ren opened the door and the swift Australian shepherd returned to forge a gap through the gathering crowd. Harold raced in arcs behind us, creating a wind that pushed us up the street and back to the safety of our own stores.

"*Relative* safety," Mr. Bixby said, as we came in to find Sinda sweeping up the last traces of our failed growth spell. "Here the biggest threat is yourself."

CHAPTER EIGHT

Twenty minutes later, we knocked on the door of Ronna Tweeze's apartment. Ren had been here before for a work get-together and wanted to check in on her former colleague. The colleague who just happened to have fled a suspected crime scene.

Visiting a witness before the police probably wouldn't be understandable—or acceptable—to Chief Gillock, I knew, but Mr. Bixby was all for it.

"You snooze, you lose," the dog said. "Put me down so I can do my own reconnaissance."

"Sure, but please keep quiet," I said. "As for you, Miss Bijou, I took issue with that word you used earlier."

"Good witch," Bijou said. "Protecting Renny Ren Ren."

I tried to glare at her but it was hard to be mad at a dog with such a sweet face. Bijou was just worried. She'd come back from the dead to protect Ren and it was turning out to be a big job.

"Failing," Bijou said. "Bad bad Bijou."

Renata picked up the poodle and hugged her. "You're awesome, Bijou. I love you to bits."

The door cracked open but the chain was still hooked. Ronna

peered out, with streaks of mascara and turquoise eye shadow on her cheeks. "What do you want?"

"Just checking on you," Ren said. "We saw you leaving the Beanstalk earlier. You must be so upset about what happened."

Ronna started to close the door. "I'm fine. Just go away."

"You're obviously not fine," Ren persisted. "Your makeup's always on point, Ronna. I guess that's why your tips were better than mine."

The crack widened slightly as Ronna patted her cheek with a tissue. "Your tips were good enough to escape the Beanstalk, Renata. To start your own business without Mitzy crushing your— Never mind."

"Can you let us in for just a minute or two?" Ren asked. "We want to speak privately."

There was a swish of blonde bouffant behind the chain. "Sorry, no. I'm still processing everything. It's a lot."

It wouldn't be long before nosy neighbors tuned in, so I decided to move the conversation along by touching Ronna's cool fingers as they clutched the edge of the door. She wasn't wearing jewelry, which was always my easiest ticket in, but I managed to slip past her mental barricades easily enough. Once inside, however, I found myself enveloped by a cloud of panic that kept her from thinking straight.

I tried to calm her by gently pushing a thought into her mind: "We can help."

Influencing people's thinking was complicated, especially when emotions ran high, and I was a relative novice.

"Relatively old and relatively new," Mr. Bixby said, from around my ankles. "Tough to be you, today."

It must have worked, because the chain came off and the door opened. We hurried inside before Ronna could change her mind. Drew likely wouldn't be happy we'd beaten him to the witness but if he was entertaining any notion of Ren's involvement in Mitzy's death, we had every right to do as we thought best.

"He might think differently," Bixby said, as he slipped away. "Big Red's uptight that way."

Ronna reached out to Bijou with a trembling hand. Her purple nail polish was glossy and I wondered how she maintained it in a tough job like waiting tables. A nice manicure was too much of a commitment for me now.

Renata handed the poodle right over to Ronna, despite the dog's squeak of protest. Bijou was still shy after decades of isolation in my store. She had been utterly alone most of the time, whereas Mr. Bixby had lived with Sinda and her late husband. He'd enjoyed a comparatively full life, complete with TV and movies that kept him up to date on current affairs.

Simply holding Bijou calmed Ronna immediately and noticeably. That gift wasn't really in Mr. Bixby's repertoire. He was more of a galvanizing force.

"That's because you need galvanizing," my dog called from the bedroom. "Sinda finds me delightfully calming. Better than aromatherapy, she said."

"Ronna, you're obviously rattled," Ren said. "What happened at the Beanstalk today?"

"I had a fight with Mitzy," Ronna blurted, hugging Bijou. "This morning, as soon as I clocked in."

"You never fight with Mitzy," Ren said. "And trust me, I know she deserved it sometimes with the way she spoke to you. To all of us."

"Bully," Bijou said. "Bully bully bad boss."

Ronna moved one hand from the dog to pat her hair. It looked lacquered down but had still blown around during her sprint out of the alley. For all we knew, a certain ghost sheepdog could have accelerated those sneakers. "I couldn't take it anymore, Ren. I quit today."

"Quit?" Ren asked. "That's wonderful, Ronna. I mean, I think so. Do you have a new job lined up?"

I glanced around the apartment and realized Ronna didn't have a lot of spare cash. That's probably why she'd stayed so long with a bully boss.

"Yeah, finally," Ronna said. "I've been doing this self-help course, you see. Online. Every day I have to find ten reasons I'm good enough and smart enough and worthy of being treated well." She scraped at the mascara with one purple fingernail. "I guess it's working, because when Ethan Bogart posted a 'help wanted' sign for his new bistro, I went in and applied. He hired me on the spot, and with a decent raise, too. What a sweetheart."

"Ethan?" Ren's face flushed. "Well, that's wonderful and you deserve it, Ronna. You've often run the Beanstalk when Mitzy's away."

"Never got a penny's raise in twenty years," Ronna said. "And if the cash was off by ten cents, it came out of my tips. Mitzy never appreciated me. Or any of us."

Ren reached out and patted her arm. "I know, but we escaped. Both of us. Mitzy... she didn't. Do you know what happened to her?"

The blonde bouffant nodded and then swished a negative. "Not really. It was all very strange."

"Just tell us what you know," I said, fingers twitching to find out another way.

"Easy, Witchy," Bijou said. "Let Renny-ren do her thing. Fluffy hair likes her."

I took the dog's advice and a rich voice called out from the kitchen, "So you'll listen to the poodle and not me?"

I ignored him and gave Ren a look to continue.

"So, you had a fight with Mitzy when you gave your notice," Ren prompted.

"That's right. She was so mad, Ren. She said we were betraying her. All of us. That she gave us our start and we burned her. Since Ethan announced the opening of his new restaurant, Mitzy's been beyond stressed. I got the impression money was tight, although business hadn't declined, as far as I could see. You hooked her up with another good baker and our tables were full."

"I guess it was too much change all at once," Ren said. "Mitzy was always strung pretty tight. What happened next?"

Ronna ran glossy fingertips over Bijou's apricot fluff. "Diggory Waring stopped outside the café this morning and then walked away. Mitzy figured he was going to visit you and decided to follow him. Said she was going to give you a piece of her mind. Ethan was going to get another piece on the way back."

"I got my piece," Ren said. "How long was she gone?"

"Maybe an hour, give or take," Ronna said. "It was business as usual until just before she came back, and the place suddenly emptied out. Mitzy looked around at the vacant seats and she kind of shriveled up. I thought she was going to cry for a minute. But then she turned the sign on the door to closed and told me to clock out and go home."

"And did you?" I asked.

Ronna's fluff bobbed. "Left by the back door to take out the trash, like I always do. But then I realized I'd left my phone under the cash register." Her breathing picked up. "When I went back into the kitchen, I heard Mitzy arguing with someone. I didn't want to barge in, so I just waited."

"Was it Diggs Waring?" Ren said. "The coffee beans guy?"

"That's where it gets strange." Ronna stared straight ahead and her eyes glazed. "I could only hear Mitzy's side of the argument. It was like she was talking to herself but answering someone at the same time."

"That is strange," Ren said. "What was she saying?"

"It's a bit foggy in my mind now. I think it was something like, 'You can't do that. I won't let you.' And then, 'You'll regret it.'

Mitzy's voice got louder and louder, bullying like she always does. But then her tone changed all of sudden. She got so quiet I had to —" Ronna stopped and her cheeks flushed. "I guess I shouldn't have been eavesdropping."

"You were there for a reason and tried to give her some privacy," Ren said. "What happened next?"

"Mitzy did an about-face and started to suck up to whoever it was. She said, 'You're right. I'll do whatever you want. I misspoke.'"

"And then...?" Ren prompted.

"Then there was a loud bang. Like an explosion. And Mitzy screamed. It made my ears ring and I hid behind the freezer with—"

She stopped again and this time, I stepped in to prompt Ronna. "With someone else? Was there another witness?"

Ronna's eyes cut away from us and she shook her head. "Just me. I misspoke, too."

"Spitz?" Ren asked. "Our busboy?"

Ronna shook her head harder. "It was just me. And after it got quiet, I poked my head out and saw Mitzy lying there. I knew she was—well, gone. The green light from the Beanstalk sign was flickering in her eyes. They were always like ice behind her glasses."

"Did you get your phone?" I asked.

She nodded. "Then I went back to the freezer and called the police. And then you guys came in. You know the rest."

Mr. Bixby came back from his mission. "You believe her?"

I did believe Ronna, except for the part about Spitz, the busboy.

"I'm sure the police will get to the bottom of this in no time," Ren said, trying to take Bijou back.

Ronna held onto the dog. "Ren, I think someone killed Mitzy. What if they come after me? Or us?"

This time Bijou pushed as Ren pulled, and Ronna had to let go. "From what you said, Mitzy may have had some kind of emotional breakdown and was just arguing with herself."

"But there was that big bang," Ronna said. "I smelled coffee and then... whammo."

"Maybe the espresso machine shorted," Ren said. "You know it was old and glitchy."

Ronna laced her glossy nails and wrung her hands. "Maybe. Maybe that's all it was."

"Leave it to the police," Ren said. "We'll talk to you soon. And if you remember anything else, call me, okay?"

The waitress nodded. "I'm so glad things worked out for you, Renata. It was harder for us after you left, but I still wished you the best."

Ren gave her a one-armed hug, which gave me a chance for a last glance around.

There was a tricolor flash as Harold got off the couch. This ghost seemed to be everywhere, following at will. Or leading, for that matter. With all I knew about sheepdogs, Harold could very well be running the investigation.

"Blasphemy," Mr. Bixby said, swaggering ahead of me into the hall. "Hairball may be taller, but I'm top dog, here. Don't you forget it."

CHAPTER NINE

I didn't love the idea of visiting a man named Spitz in his basement apartment alone. After dropping Ren and Sinda at the manor to wait for the police, however, I told them I was going to pick up some groceries and set off to beat Drew to the punch with another witness.

"You're never alone when there's a pedigreed dachshund dangling under your arm like a designer purse," Mr. Bixby said, as I paused at the top of the cement staircase. "I'm sure Mr. Spitz will be awed by my presence."

There was refuse on every stair, including scattered beer cans. I wasn't convinced Spitz would be impressed by either of us. We probably weren't his type of people.

"Hate to break it to you, but we aren't people," Bixby said. "I'm surprised by how often you lump yourself in with ordinary mortals. You could turn this fellow into a blithering fool with a poke from your pinkie."

"But I don't want to operate that way. It attracts attention. I spent my whole life as a—"

"Smooth operator?" Bixby offered.

"I suppose, yeah. Ivy Galloway called me 'Janelle Bond,' and I liked it." I sighed as I took the first step down. "Now, here I am in Mom's frumpy dress and rubber-soled heels, and all the rules have changed."

"You've changed, too. Anyone who put someone like Oscar Knight on notice should have more confidence. Maybe you need to take that self-development course Ronna mentioned. She probably had a harsh, critical mother, too."

I laughed. "I'll put self-development on my to-do list. Right under opening the store and learning to harness my power to stun."

"Don't forget spelling for the win," he said. "Unless you enjoy killing innocent sunflowers."

"I don't enjoy killing anything, especially not flowers. We need more beauty in this world."

"Okay, beautiful, stop stalling and start walking. Don't stumble on a beer can on the way down."

"Janelle Bond never stumbles in heels," I said, more for my own benefit than his. "I glide over the detritus of life."

"Poetry in motion. As your handbag, I would know."

Spitz didn't open the door on the first knock or the second. I could feel his presence, however, even through the metal. There was a frenetic energy behind the door that confirmed we'd come to the right place for a new perspective on a difficult situation. But I wouldn't get that perspective if he didn't let me in.

"Sweet-talk him," Bixby said, using our inside channel. "Use the silver tongue you brag about."

"I don't brag. Well, not as much as you, anyway."

He chuckled. "If you're in competition with a formerly dead dachshund, I don't like our chances of making it big in this town."

Ignoring him, I straightened my shoulders and pulled out my best hospitality voice. "Mr. Spitz? I know you're home and I'd appreciate a word with you. My name is Janelle Brighton and our mutual friend Renata Scott sent me over."

The door stayed closed but the doorknob jiggled slightly, as if he were considering my request.

"Ren and I aren't friends," he called through the door. "Not anymore. She left us behind like trash and moved up in the world with you."

I glanced around at the litter again and realized how often the outside world represented our inner landscape.

"Exactly," Bixby said. "That's why I recommend a style upgrade. Wearing your Mom's castoffs sends the wrong message... to yourself."

Resting my open palm on the door, I tried again. "Well, Renata still thinks fondly of you, Mr. Spitz. She said you were an incredibly hard worker destined for greater things than the Beanstalk Café."

"I don't work there anymore. And I don't want to talk about it."

He was resolute and with a metal door between us, there was little I could do about it. Soon, our voices would attract attention from the street above, and the police would hear about my visit sooner than I would like.

"Spitz, come on," I said. "Ren needs your help."

There was a long pause, during which I stared at the doorknob, and then finally a "Nope. I don't owe her anything."

A stiff wind came up behind me and the trash whirled off the stairs and into a vortex on the lower landing. Crushed beer cans hit the metal door with a clatter, one after the other.

"What are you doing?" he called.

"Nothing." I shielded my face. "The wind's come up, that's all. I'd love to step inside. It's making a mess of my hair and dress."

The appeal to chivalry failed, and with it the patience of the wind-maker. Harold, the Australian shepherd, took the stairs at a bound and passed right through the metal door.

"I hate it when he does that," Mr. Bixby said. "In my day, ghosts had a certain decorum. He thinks he's hot—"

"Never mind," I told him. "It's working."

The door opened suddenly and a windblown young man stood in the doorway looking startled. "I could feel it inside," he said. "It's like a tornado."

Without waiting for an invitation, I slid through the gap and stood in a surprisingly neat little unit. He didn't have a lot of belongings and everything seemed to have a place. A slightly battered loveseat was just big enough for a reclining Aussie who looked mighty pleased with himself.

"Thanks for seeing me," I said, turning on my smile. "Is Spitz your first name or your last?"

"Neither," he said, closing the door. "It's Mike Spenser. Spitz is a nickname for a bad habit I dropped last year when I turned eighteen."

He had a slight lisp and I wondered if it was caused by the small barbell visible in his tongue. There was another in his heavy, dark eyebrow. Despite the piercings, and an array of tattoos, his clothes were conservative. He was wearing dark jeans, a striped shirt and a black leather belt that matched his boots. It seemed like Spitz was a man in transition from punk to presentable.

"Well, Mike, I'm pleased to meet you. If you no longer work at the Beanstalk Café, do you have a new gig?"

He ran a hand over a quarter inch of dark stubble on his head. "Yeah. I'll be working for Ethan Bogart at his new place. Got a promotion to waiter, so I'm trying to clean up. Better for tips."

"Makes complete sense," I said. "And congratulations. How did Mitzy Lennox feel about the news?"

He eyed me cagily. "I already know you talked to Ronna Tweeze. We're friends, you know. Study buddies."

My hospitality smile turned curious. "Study buddies? I like the sound of that."

He leaned against the wall in the entry. "Ronna helped me see I was holding myself back. Keeping myself small with limiting beliefs. So we started working a program together."

Mr. Bixby gave a chuckle, and I ignored it.

"That's amazing, Mike. All the more so given you were working for someone who could be difficult. Or so Renata says."

His eyebrows came down, bringing the little barbell along for the ride. "I try not to hold it against Mitzy. Resentment is like poison. Maybe she was doing the best she could, but it wasn't good enough for me, anymore. Ethan is open to letting me grow, so I'm giving up all my jobs to focus on getting things right."

"All your jobs? How many are there?"

He shrugged, the movement revealing more of the tattoo around his neckline. It looked like a curling tail. A rat perhaps.

"Nice," Mr. Bixby said. "You know I was bred to hunt—"

I shushed him internally as Mike counted on his fingers and then said, "Five. I do cleanup at Matilda's salon, the pet store and a couple more places. But I gave proper notice to everyone today. Trying to leave on a good note." After a moment he sighed. "Didn't go over well with anyone, but Mitzy especially."

"It's a shame she wanted to hold you back," I said. "What happened?"

He ran one hand after the other over his scalp. "Hissy fit. Massive. Said we were driving her into the poorhouse. In retrospect, Ronna and I should have spaced things out more. But my shift started later and I gave my notice while Ronna was serving customers. Seemed like Mitzy was reeling. Felt bad for her, even though she was bad for us."

"I heard she was a bully. And I've worked for a few of those, so I know it takes a toll."

"Massive," he said again. "If it weren't for my other jobs, and that online class, I probably would have been stuck here forever." He waved around the basement apartment. "I plan to look out at street level one day."

"I know how he feels," Mr. Bixby said. "Maybe I should take this woo-woo course. Grow some legs."

I pressed my lips together to hold back a smirk.

"What?" Mike said. "You're thinking it's woo-woo, right? I did, too, but I'm telling you, lady, you can reprogram your unconscious beliefs."

Leaning against the wall opposite, I said, "Tell me more. I have some limiting beliefs, too, trust me."

"Critical parents, am I right? Mine thought I was destined for a hole in the ground just like this. I leave the beer cans outside to throw them off if they even consider bringing their bad vibes here. And every day, I think of 10 ways I've proven I'm not what they told me. I'm good enough, I'm smart enough and I deserve to live upstairs."

"All true," I said. "I can tell, and I've only known you a few minutes. Don't let anyone say otherwise."

His upper barbell took the ride down to a scowl. "That's why I'm home today. I figured if I got caught up in what happened, it would undo all my work. And I didn't do anything wrong."

"You were with Ronna when things exploded at the Beanstalk."

"Yeah. We were stuck in the kitchen and part of me wanted to go out to interrupt the argument. Be a hero. But if I stick my head up, I'm the type of guy who gets it shot off."

"Used to be. Not anymore," I said. "Just the same, it was probably a smart move. Ronna said things got heated between Mitzy and someone else. What did you hear?"

The cagey look came back. "Why should I tell you? A complete stranger?"

"Because I'm Renata's best friend, and we showed up in the wrong place at the wrong time. The police found us there and they know about Mitzy having words with Ren. Jimmy Barrow suggested she's a suspect. But I say Mitzy just got hit with bad luck."

His lips pursed. "She got hit with something and it smelled like burnt coffee."

"First, she argued with someone, though, right?"

The rise and fall of his shoulders revealed even more of the tattoo. Maybe it wasn't a rat, after all. "I didn't hear anything but the big bang. When I saw how Mitzy landed, I didn't stick around. Tried to get Ronna to come with me but she wanted to grab her phone."

Mike liked to talk, as it turned out, but he wasn't as easy to steer as I'd expected. I'd need to try something new.

"Bold idea," Mr. Bixby said. "How about using the gifts you were born with? Touch something and make it quick."

I directed an internal sigh at the dog. "What, exactly? His hand? His eyebrow stud? Isn't that going to look a little forward?"

"There's the barbell in his tongue. You could try that."

"Then I'd have to kiss him. Are you serious, Bixby?"

He chuckled again. "What's a little smooch for our good friend, Ren?"

"Not a chance," I muttered internally. "There's got to be a better way."

Mike straightened and pushed himself off the wall. "I used to do that, you know. Ruminate. Hold all these arguments with myself. There's a better way. You can learn it, too."

"I want to hear more about this course you're taking," I said. "But first, I want to say I like that little barbell in your eyebrow. I've been thinking of getting something like that. Maybe a blingy stud."

The barbell soared and he grinned. "I've got a stud with topaz right here." He slapped his chest. "Going to keep that one and let the others grow in."

"Better for tips," I said.

"Exactly. No one sees the topaz." He gave me a surprisingly bashful smile. "Not right now, anyway. Waiting to start dating till I have my act together."

Mr. Bixby cleared his throat. "At the risk of sounding crass, Miss Brighton, it sounds like Spitz here has a nice gem in his chesticle. Topaz is right up your alley, magically speaking."

"Bixby, no. I absolutely refuse to cross that line."

That's when the wind came up again, and in the tiny apartment, it was a veritable cyclone. A gust forced me away from the wall and tossed me against Mike like a crushed beer can. I managed to hold on to Bixby and get my other hand up in time.

Fingers splayed out against Mike's chest, I blinked a few times as the wind died down. I knew what he'd tried to avoid saying: that Mitzy had been arguing not with herself, but someone else. Possibly a man, although things got decidedly hazy in Mike's memory after that. There may have been magical mental tampering to blur the details.

Before I could try to pluck any more information out of him, the young man politely disconnected me from his topaz stud.

"It's the shirt," Bixby said. "Maybe if you—"

I stepped away. "Mike, I'm so sorry. I lost my balance in that breeze."

"With all due respect," he said. "Are you hitting on me?"

"Of course not. I'm old enough to be your— your aunt."

He laughed and his teeth were surprisingly nice. "Dude, no. I like cougars."

I gave up on learning more about the argument. Harold had decided I had all I needed, apparently, because the breeze blew in a half circle around me, driving me to the door.

"Thanks so much, Mike," I said. "Good luck with your new job."

"Wait," he called after me as I raced up the stairs. "Let's be study buddies. Take things up a level."

"Dude," Mr. Bixby said, so bemused he had to speak the word aloud. "I'm about to change my mind about Harold and his windy ways."

CHAPTER TEN

Renata and Sinda were sitting at the kitchen table drinking tea when I walked into the manor later. We had agreed to stay there together until the latest trouble blew over, so to speak.

"You just missed Andrew," Sinda said, stirring more milk into her tea. "I daresay he was disappointed. Asked a few too many questions about your whereabouts."

"Luckily, we didn't know so we didn't need to lie," Ren said.

"We visited the Beanstalk's former busboy," I said. "And after that I took a walk to recover my dignity." I responded to Bixby's gesture to be set on the counter. My dog always preferred to be closer to eye level, or at least away from shoes. My footsteps were a little too agitated for his liking right now. "That young man thinks I hit on him."

"Spitz?" Ren said. "You're old enough to be his—"

"Aunt," I interrupted. "But he's fine with cougars, apparently."

Mr. Bixby cocked his head, which I was beginning to see as equivalent to a smile. "Dude needs to sign up for my personal development course. He's selling himself short."

"Mr. Bixby, that's awful," Ren said. "Spitz would be so lucky to get Janelle."

Sinda smiled over her teacup. "Particularly since Drew's already got her."

"I don't know about that," I said. "But I do know that Harold blew me into a somewhat compromising position."

I shook my finger at the ghost Aussie, who was perched on one of the high stools at the kitchen counter. There was nowhere he couldn't go, apparently. Someone had figured out how to break all the rules with this ghost. It was just as well Sir Nigel wasn't at home, because it might have stirred his ambitions. Our butler was at the mercy of Mom's rules and she kept his life fairly circumscribed.

Mr. Bixby chuckled as I described the unprofessional interview to Ren and Sinda. Then he strutted across the kitchen counter to meet Harold's supposedly vacant eyes. "Dude," Mr. Bixby said. "I'm sorry I was rude earlier. You're welcome to blow things up if you keep me entertained."

"There are better ways to investigate," I said, walking over to the espresso maker. It was a miniature version of the one in Ren's new store. Normally I'd make myself a coffee but my stomach gave a little twist that drove me to the refrigerator instead. It had been thoroughly cleaned several times since Mom came home after her extended stay in the bunker, but I still didn't trust it. Mostly, I'd been eating takeout at the store, which gave me the added benefit of avoiding both Mom and Boz.

In the end, I just grabbed a glass and used the water and ice dispensers on the front of the fridge.

"No luck at the salon or pet store," I said. "The police were already there."

"What about Diggory Waring and Norm Jenkins?" Ren asked. "If Spitz heard a male voice, it most likely belonged to one of them."

"I tried texting Norm but he didn't answer," I said. "We might have better luck with the ladies. They may have seen something."

"But why wouldn't Ronna have heard this argument?" Ren asked.

"Maybe Mike has more magic in him than it seemed." I sighed. "I was too flustered to do my best work."

"Don't count out your charm because of one misfire," Bixby said. "You'll get your groove back."

I deliberately turned my back on him and paced the kitchen. "Did you learn anything new from Drew?"

Ren shook her head. "Not really, but I sense he believes I had nothing to do with this. Jimmy Barrow and Chief Dredger are coming around tomorrow and they probably won't be as kind. I don't understand it. Jimmy used to be so fond of me."

Sighing, I set my elbows on the cool marble counter and rested my chin in my hands. "It's your proximity to me, most likely. My family. My reputation."

"And now your standoff with Oscar Knight," Mr. Bixby added helpfully. "That's probably made a few waves."

"Whose side are you on?" I asked, squinting at him.

He let his ears flop fetchingly. "Depends. Which dog is your favorite?"

"Me," Bijou said, prancing. "Pick me-me-me."

Sinda and Ren both laughed, and I couldn't help joining them. "You're taken, my poodle friend, but I love you, too. Plenty to go around. Even for Harold if he's open to it."

The sheepdog's expression didn't change. To me, it was deliberately neutral, rather than vacant. I suspected he had been very well trained by someone, and I hoped I'd have a chance to thank them. This dog was herding me through some tricky situations with speed, if not elegance.

My phone rang. After checking the screen, I put it on speaker and set it on the counter. "Hey, Gran! We're all here. Sinda, Ren and the dogs."

"I didn't say you could have a party." The voice was Mom's, but there was a smile in it. "I'm glad you're not alone after what happened."

"And I'm glad you arrived safely. Did your own phone break?"

"Just wanted to be sure you'd pick up," she said, laughing.

"That trick will only work once," I told her. "We're onto you."

"You'll always take Gran's calls. Her ratings are consistently high."

There was no point disputing it. Gran had always been the most important person in my life.

"Until I came along," Bixby said, silently for a change. "I'm vying for top dog."

"I'm right here, Janny," Gran called. "Be warned. We've had a glass of bubbly."

Mom and Gran were drinking together? That could either go very well or spectacularly badly. Neither imbibed normally, but emotions were probably still running high over their reunion.

"Where's Boz?" I asked. "He doesn't approve of alcohol."

"Drove to the beach," Mom said. "He doesn't feel the heat like I do."

"And he's not afraid of alligators, like I am," Gran added.

"We wouldn't have popped the cork had we known about Mitzy, of course," Mom said. "Let alone what happened at Ren's store. Luckily, I have a few tricks up my sleeve for picking up news. So, I'll turn around and come home tomorrow. Can you stay out of trouble till then?"

"No," Mr. Bixby said, very much aloud this time. "What fun would that be?"

Mom laughed again. "Bixby, can I trust you to keep them safe?"

"I'm on it, Shelley. It's a big job for a small dog, but I'm ambitious."

"He's got some backup," I said. "From the ghost dog who turned up at Whimsy today."

"Another one?" The apprehension in Mom's voice was obvious. "Aren't they harbingers of trouble?"

"I beg your pardon?" Bixby sounded prickly. "I turned up to help Janelle when she was already in trouble."

"Let me rephrase that," Mom said. "Don't these appearances generally *coincide* with problems? How is it that this dog turned up on the same day Mitzy died?"

"I don't know," I said. "But Harold's been nothing but helpful so far. He's an Australian sheepdog with some interesting abilities. He isn't bound to the store, for example. And he whirls up wind with his herding moves."

"Harold? That's an unusual name," Mom said.

"Not in my day," Gran chipped in. "I knew a couple of Harolds, or Harrys."

I took a closer look at the Aussie. "Gran, he's wearing a distinctive tag. It looks like an inverted toadstool. Does that ring any bells?"

"Ah yes, the toadstool era," Gran said. "Right around the time you were born, the township changed Wyldwood's branding to exploit the magical element. Toadstools and cauldrons and even peaked hats started appearing on signage. But then the powers that be changed their minds just as suddenly and nixed the whole experiment. A more sensible mayor took office and the town's been quite conservative ever since."

"Ruthann Longmuir," Mom said. "Never thought much of her. Lives in Oscar's pocket."

I tipped my head at Harold and he mirrored my pose. "So that means Harold was probably living in Wyldwood thirty years ago, give or take. Maybe I can figure out where he really belongs and why he's here."

"Or you could focus on keeping Ren and yourself out of hot water in a boiling cauldron," Mom said. "We have bigger fish to fry than a herding ghost dog."

"Aren't you mixing your metaphors?" I asked.

"Aren't you hiding the fact you had a magical misfire today?" she countered.

"Mom! Do you have a camera on Whimsy? That's a total invasion of my privacy."

She didn't deny it. "I didn't let you have a lock on your bedroom door for this very reason. You said you wouldn't go spelling and went ahead and did it."

"Never said I wouldn't. I stopped following orders when I was seventeen."

"Easy, girls," Gran said. "Everyone agrees Janny needs to gain mastery over her powers. She gets to decide when and how that happens. Whether we like it or not, Shelley, our children grow up. If we've done the job right, they have minds of their own."

Mom let out a huffy grumble and then spoke up again. "What happened today proved my point."

"It was just a simple growth spell," I said. "Sinda got a pretty gerbera out of it."

"Before its fiery demise," Mom said. "Alongside yours and Ren's. Meanwhile, down the road, someone else ended with a spark and a sputter. According to my sources."

Leaving the phone on the counter, I started pacing. "Are you implying our growth spell had something to do with Mitzy's death?"

"It wouldn't be the first time your power has had unexpected consequences."

I did two complete turns of the kitchen, musing. "But Mitzy was blocks away at the time. Isn't it more likely someone rigged her espresso machine?"

"Isn't it possible someone used a means of dispensing with Mitzy that might frame you with the magical police? Have you considered Ren isn't the primary target, but collateral damage? Oscar Knight wouldn't hesitate to do such a thing if he thought he could get away with it."

"It was a growth spell." My voice was plaintive, as if I were a kid who'd been caught turning rocks into donuts. "Beginner level stuff."

Gran stepped into the fray. "I'm not sure I understand any of this. Shelley, are you saying someone hijacked Janny's spell? Have you ever heard of such a thing happening before?"

There was a long pause. "Not like that, I suppose," Mom said. "I don't believe there's a magical precedent."

I continued to pace, missing my stilettos. A proper click did so much more to relieve tension than the slight thud of Mom's borrowed rubber-tipped heels. "Without magical precedent. Just like Bixby."

"And the rest of your growing pack," Mom said.

There was a tinkle of bottle against glass on her end. Someone found the notion warranted more alcohol.

"Perhaps Janny herself is without magical precedent," Gran said.

I scooped Mr. Bixby off the counter and resumed pacing. "I don't feel good about that."

"Nor do I," Mom said. "Rules generally work for us, like dance steps. They keep things organized. When we're freestyling, people start smashing into each other like pinballs." She paused and then added, "And yes, I'm mixing my metaphors. Blame it on the bubbly."

"Maybe you had better go home, Shelley," Gran said. "I don't want Janny freestyling alone and getting smashed like a pinball."

I stopped walking. "Gran, I don't want you getting smashed by buses in Strathmore County. Mom needs to get that sorted out. In the meantime, I have plenty of help here. I just need to—"

"Stay away from your spell book," Mom said. "And Oscar Knight."

"Haven't seen him in three weeks," I said. "I really think I'm off his radar."

Her next laugh had a cynical edge. "You outwitted him once, Janelle. His pride won't ever let you off his radar. His first thought every morning will be about regaining the upper hand."

"This is one circumstance where staying small might be a good idea," Gran said.

"I take issue with that remark," Bixby said.

I knew he would and counted on him to spare me the energy. After more than a decade on the run I hadn't come home to stay small. Clearly, however, I'd have to figure out a more skillful way to grow than my simple spell.

"Mom, we'll be more careful. If I had something to do with what happened to Mitzy, I don't want to get anywhere near the spell book."

"Let Chief Gillock work the official channels," Gran said. "Perhaps your mother can pull a few strings from here."

"I'll try," Mom said. "Unfortunately, I've burned some bridges in Wyldwood."

Harold jumped down from the stool and whirled around to let me know the time for family bonding had come to an end. He was a dog of action.

I said my goodbyes but Gran held me back a moment. "Be careful whose toes you dance on, Janny."

"Careful with the bubbly, Gran," I replied. "Harder to evade rogue buses when you're tipsy."

CHAPTER ELEVEN

The shadows were getting long when Ren, Sinda and I drove toward town later. Fall was very much in the air now, and I didn't particularly relish winter in Wyldwood Springs. The pretty waterfalls rarely froze but the mist made everything slippery and it was difficult to get around in nice footwear. Rugged boots were likely to be my only option.

"Probably wise when everyone wants to dance on your toes," Bixby said, from Sinda's lap in the passenger seat.

"I wish I could always hear both sides of the conversation," Sinda said. "You two seem to have such fun."

Reaching out, I scratched Bixby's ears. "He keeps me sharp. There's little time to overthink when you're never alone in your own mind."

"You're alone in there more than I'd like," he said. "Every day you get a little better at blocking me out."

"It's just part of the process, I guess. What process, I'm not sure."

"Metamorphosis," Sinda suggested.

"Evolution," Ren added from the back seat.

"Mastery." Bixby's voice had an air of finality. "I understand it, so I only take it personally part of the time."

"We've all just begun, really," Sinda said. "Ren and I have even more to learn than you, Janelle, and no mother to guide us."

I turned the car onto Main Street. "There's plenty of Mom to go around. Since she's aware she burned bridges, she'll be happy to build some new ones."

"Her bridge with me is solid," Ren said, from the back seat. "She was so good to me while you were gone, Janny."

"I'm glad to hear it, although sometimes I think we're talking about two different people."

Taking a right turn off Main Street, I found a relatively sheltered parking spot. My only complaint about Elsa was that she was distinctive, which made sneaking around difficult. I turned the key and then patted the dash for what felt like a disloyal thought. This car had been my only friend for a long time, and briefly my home.

"Times have changed," Bixby said, letting me pluck him from Sinda's lap. "Rather remarkably, it seems."

"Some things stay the same," I said, getting out of the car and joining the others to walk back to Main Street. "Including the need for good hair."

Matilda Wentwhistle's chubby cheeks seemed to deflate as we walked through the door at A Cut Above. "We're closed," she said, ending with a squawk as a stiff breeze hit her and pushed her back toward the two styling chairs. Harold jumped into one of them and settled with his paws crossed.

"The open sign is still on," I said. "And I've never needed a blowout more."

"Me either," Ren said, clawing at her long locks. "It's been so windy today. My hair's in perpetual tangles."

Sinda patted her short hair. "Between the dampness and the breeze, mine is constantly limp. Good hair is so very critical to mental wellness, isn't it?"

"So critical," I echoed. "And after a day like today, we need all the help we can get."

Matilda's small eyes narrowed. "You're complaining? Mitzy Lennox doesn't have the luxury of worrying about her hair anymore."

"It's a terrible shame what happened," I said. "We heard she took a fall in the café."

Her lips curled in scorn. "I know you were at the Beanstalk, Janelle. Everyone does. And we also know you gave Mitzy a heart attack."

"Me? Why would you say that?"

"Renata wouldn't be in a position to open her bakery if you hadn't manipulated Oscar Knight. And Oscar wouldn't have raised our rents if you hadn't stolen part of his income stream. I had to let a stylist go to make up the difference and Mitzy was struggling to make ends meet."

"She saved some money from my salary," Ren said. "The baker she commissioned charges far less."

Matilda pursed her lips. "It wasn't enough. And the remaining staff wanted raises. They stabbed her in the back, you know. Two of them quit today. It broke Mitzy's heart."

"How is it that Ren and I are getting all the blame in the court of public opinion?" I asked, walking over to a mirror and scowling at my reflection. My curls truly were windblown and matted. Harold might be protecting me but I was paying a price in vanity.

"If you two hadn't followed Mitzy back to the Beanstalk and yelled at her, she'd still be here," Matilda said. "Probably."

I sat down on the styling chair Harold wasn't occupying and pushed off in a spin. During my childhood, I always had my hair cut here but there was no way I'd let Matilda near me with scissors now. "That's not what happened. I never got a chance to tell Mitzy off for being so harsh with Ren."

Pulling a long metal comb out of her smock pocket, Matilda

jabbed it in my direction. "That's not what I heard. Mitzy was screaming at someone and felt under attack."

I assumed the seed for this story came from Ronna Tweeze. My name had conveniently been inserted into the one-sided conversation.

"There's a video camera on the front door of the café," Ren said. "The police will find we arrived after Mitzy passed."

I suspected that camera was conveniently on the fritz. Otherwise, the police would probably have made an arrest already. Things were never that easy in Wyldwood.

"Then maybe Janelle yelled at her over the phone. I don't know the exact details. But I do know that between the two of you, Mitzy's dead. Maybe you were aiming to take over the Beanstalk instead of launching your own place, Ren."

"You're really grasping, Matilda," Ren said. "I'm thrilled to co-own my new space. But maybe someone else wanted Mitzy's store. Especially if she was having money trouble."

If I hadn't already chatted to Ronna and Mike, they would be my first suspects. Each was looking for a fresh start and may well have wanted to run a café. But I'd touched both and would very likely have detected murderous intent.

"It sounds like the stress just got too much for Mitzy," I said. "That's so sad, no matter what happened."

As I spun the chair again, she shook her comb at me. "People are suggesting foul play, you know. I've never believed you didn't kill Loretta Billings."

Stopping the spin with my foot, I stared at her. "Even though someone else confessed? And is doing jail time?"

"Who's suggesting foul play?" Ren asked.

The comb jabbed in her direction. "Everyone, that's who. Mitzy walked in the hills every day and ate her greens. There's no way she had a heart attack."

I got out of the chair. "What are folks saying?"

Her comb dangled in mid-air and then dropped to her side. "There was a loud noise. A bang. Gus Weeble from the hardware store said the place shook till tools fell off the pegboard. And Kathleen at the dry cleaners said she smelled smoke."

"Anything else?" I asked.

"Coffee," Matilda said. "The whole town smelled like roasting beans today. Thick and heavy. Kathleen said she felt drowsy and had a little nap right at the counter."

Ren's eyebrows shot up. "Really? I counted on coffee—even the smell—to keep me awake when I worked at the Beanstalk. As a baker, I'm an early riser."

The stylist shrugged and the comb twitched uneasily. "Gus said the same thing. At first he was worried about the bang and then felt sort of mellow about it. Normally people are pretty quick to call the cops but it didn't even occur to them to go over and check on Mitzy."

Mr. Bixby stirred in my arms, and then used his inside voice to say, "The plot thickens... with enchanted coffee. Why didn't it affect Ronna and Spitz the same way? Not to mention you and your friends?"

They were good questions. Maybe it was because the door to the alley was open and aired the place out? Or maybe Ronna and Mike had some magical immunity. That would likely be the case for Sinda, Ren and me.

Matilda walked over and touched the door handle. "I really am closed, ladies," she said. "I can hardly hold a comb steady. You wouldn't want me detangling today, let alone styling."

If I had any doubt about our business being done, the little whirlwind of hair clippings that swept up assured me. All of us sneezed, including the two dogs. Harold faked one, just to keep us company.

"Another time," Ren said, leading us out with Bijou. "It was nice talking to you, Matilda."

The stylist tried to push the door closed behind me. "I wish I could say the same. And for your information, I told the police everything I know. Officer Barrow wanted *all* the details."

She dragged out the "all" for strategic effect.

Even before we were out of earshot, Mr. Bixby turned in my arms to glance at Ren and said, "Young Jimmy seems way too interested in the case. Maybe Janelle's not our only cougar."

Renata laughed, but Bijou air-snapped around my knees. "Come down here and say that, wiener boy. Easy to be snarky when you're always riding high."

"Speaking of high," I said, over Bixby's chuckle, "I wonder what Jimmy's going to make of enchanted coffee fumes. Because it sure seems like someone's staging a magical coverup of what transpired at the Beanstalk."

The dachshund struggled to get down and then vied for the lead on the sidewalk with the lanky poodle. "Hopefully Jimmy got a big hit of happy and is home sleeping it off right now."

"If only it were that simple," Ren said. "Jimmy's trying to make a name for himself in a town where everyone still thinks of him as a kid. Proving me guilty might make him feel he's graduated to the big leagues."

I patted her arm. "He can't prove anything, don't worry. That's why we're out here beating the pavement. We need to find some leads before Drew catches up to us and creates roadblocks."

Sinda touched Ren's arm. "Have you seen any more auras? It seemed like a promising beginning."

"A promising beginning that fizzled," Ren said. "Even you two look normal again."

"Shame," I said. "I like the idea of walking in a rainbow."

Bijou was hauling Ren along like a sled dog just to make Bixby work harder. I didn't carry a leash because his paws so rarely touched down. Besides, this doxy didn't plan to be led.

"It's your fault I'm unfit," he called back to me, puffing. "I used to be a fine athlete. A killer of—"

"We only want to focus on one killer right now," I interrupted. "If you two can't sort out your discord, I'm sure Harold will lend a hand."

Both dogs settled immediately. The tornados the herding dog created were strong enough to move humans around. Two smaller dogs could be blown clear to Oz.

"Calm yourself, Bijou," Bixby said, circling back to my ankles. "Perhaps it's best we join forces to get rid of the windy one."

"Ya-ya-ya," Bijou said. "He's an ill wind that blows no good."

"Harold's doing us all some good," I assured the perky poodle. "Possibly Ren most of all."

CHAPTER TWELVE

When we reached Small Wonders, Becca Mathews was desperately trying to flip the lock and the sign to closed at the same time. The tremble in the cardboard told me she'd received a heads-up from her friend Matilda and was anxious to avoid our visit.

I managed to press the door open just enough to shove Mom's sensible shoe into the gap. My toes had frequently suffered from being pinched in fine footwear but now their sacrifice was nobler.

"Just in time," I said. "Whew! We're out of dog food, Becca. Could have been a canine crisis."

She wanted to hold out but depriving pets of food wouldn't be good for business. Besides, I could tell just from brushing her fingertips that her love of animals was genuine. That feeling didn't necessarily extend to people, and I couldn't blame her. It was hard to know who to trust in Wyldwood and her posse was down by one today.

Standing back, she let us pass. Harold made his own way in and frolicked around the store as if enjoying the modern perks of pet life. There were toys and treats such as he could never have known as a dog living 30 years ago.

Bixby's muzzle followed for a moment. "I remember that feeling. Wait till Hairball can smell again. His senses will overload."

Becca snapped her fingers to get my attention. "If you could hurry, I'd appreciate it, ladies. The police only just left and I'm tired."

"Understandable, and we're sorry for your loss," I said. Harold herded Sinda, Ren and Bijou into the kibble aisle, so I assumed he was delegating the interrogation to me. "What a terrible shock for you."

"Terrible," she agreed, walking around the counter to the cash register. "Mitzy and I were friends longer than you've been on the planet."

Bending, I lifted Mr. Bixby and set him on the counter. This was one of the few places we didn't need to ask permission. Becca reached out to pat him and while my dog didn't encourage liberties, he took it like a champ for the cause. Perhaps his silky fur would ease Becca's grief and loosen her tongue.

I gave her time for a couple of head-to-tail runs over Bixby and then took my chance. "If you knew Mitzy that well, I suppose you were aware she was under a lot of stress."

Her eyes lifted from the dog and pinned me over the heavy dark frames of her glasses. "How would you know anything about Mitzy's stress levels?"

"It was pretty obvious when you visited Renata's store this morning. I've also known Mitzy since I was a kid and she was never so—"

"Mean," Bixby said.

"Agitated," I finished. "That had to be about more than Ren's leaving."

Her eyes drifted to the cash register and her fingers moved to the keys. "I've lost staff, too, and it always hurts. Our stores are like our children, as you'll soon discover, I suppose. We defend them strongly when they're threatened."

I nodded. "I already had to leap to Whimsy's defense when Oscar Knight tried to revoke my lease. He has the power to make or break any business, it seems."

Her fingers froze. Mr. Bixby walked over and nudged them until they started scratching his ears. "That's something you don't need to worry about after buying your building, Janelle. Few of us have your resources."

"I was very lucky to have backers," I said. "But that doesn't mean Oscar can't harm us in other ways. He's the king of Main Street."

"Careful," Bixby said, tipping his head to offer more ear to Becca. "Your words will get back to him and get his wand in a knot."

The dog was right and I realized I must be tired, too. I was losing my subtlety. Clearing my throat, I added, "That didn't come out right, Becca. I'm really just saying I know what you mean. I've got a motherly feeling about my store already. At least, I assume that's what it is, since I'm not actually a mother."

Becca cracked a small smile. "Well, I am. And a grandmother, too. So I can say with some authority that the feeling is probably more similar than it should be. When you invest so much time and energy into something, getting attached is inevitable."

"I suppose we can feel the same way about staff, too. When they leave the nest, it hurts."

She nodded. "Sometimes. The good ones, anyway. Mitzy took a few hits lately and she blamed Ren for starting it all. Until your friend quit, Mitzy had almost no staff turnover. That sort of stability is hard to find."

"It felt like a betrayal," I prompted.

"Very much so. Good help is hard to find in this town. There's increasing competition and costs are going up. I think it just all came together like the perfect storm for Mitzy today." She lifted her eyes from the dog again. "For what it's worth, I tried to stop her from coming. Sometimes we need to back our friends even when they're taking the wrong path."

"I know. Ultimately it was her decision." I picked up a little flashlight with a dachshund on the side. I hadn't been aware of how popular dachshunds were until I had one of my own. Now I saw them everywhere. "What happened after you left? Mitzy still had a head of steam over Rare Earth and the coffee beans. Did you all walk back to the café together?"

Becca started to nod but then her gray brows furrowed. "Actually, I stopped at the vet's office to pick up some pills for my basset hound. And Matilda went into the convenience store. She figured Mitzy might want a cigarette. I'm afraid we all started smoking again recently."

"And then you joined Mitzy afterward? I'm sure you wanted to offer more support."

Her eyes glazed as she reviewed her day. "I gave Mitzy enough time to sort things out with Diggory Waring privately and then went over to find out what happened."

"Were they still arguing when you got there?"

Her fingers hung over Bixby and I saw nicotine stains. The habit probably wasn't as new as she let on. "I'm not sure. The sign said closed and the door was locked. It was strange because she'd left Ronna in charge and I can't remember Mitzy ever closing early."

"Did you try calling her?"

"I don't think so, no."

The confusion in her eyes intensified, probably because calling was something she would normally do.

"Maybe you did," I said. "And now you've forgotten. Everyone was so flustered."

Her phone was sitting beside the cash register and Mr. Bixby gave it a poke with his nose to make it spin.

Taking the hint, Becca tapped in her password and swiped a

few times. "You're right! I did call Mitzy. Twice. And texted a few times. Why don't I remember that?"

"Because you were worried. Happens to all of us when our good friends are upset."

She stared at me, blinking rapidly. "It's the strangest thing. I don't recall anything after finding the door locked."

"Did you hear the bang?" I asked. "Everyone's talking about it."

"No bang. I guess I just came back here and fell into my usual routine. When you've been in business as long as I have, it's automatic."

Her fingers dropped to the dog again, as if satisfied with her conclusion.

Mr. Bixby turned his brown eyes on me. "Rapid heart rate. Shallow breathing. Diamond ring. Maybe put those together and do your thing."

Now I took his hint and reached over to squeeze Becca's hand. She pulled away immediately but not before I heard it.

The bang was so loud in my head that I flinched. And then Bixby flinched, because it was in his head, too. He followed that with his signature retching sound, as if he detected a sulphurous gust from Becca's memory.

The pet store owner had been holding the door at the exact moment of the blast. In my mind, I saw that diamond ring release the door handle as if it were white hot. She reached for her phone and Mitzy's voice came up faintly in voicemail. Perhaps the bang had been loud enough to make Becca's ears ring.

After that, her memory dissolved into mist.

The strangest thing of all was that I could smell coffee. Even *taste* coffee. And since there was none around, it had to come from Becca's memory.

She shook off my hand as Harold herded the others back out of the aisle. Ren was carrying a bag of kibble and Bijou seemed almost aloft from the force of the ghost dog's breeze.

Becca's eyes were still glassy as she rang up the purchase and made change for the bills Ren offered. It really did seem as if she were on automatic pilot.

"Are you feeling okay, Becca?" Ren asked, putting coins back in her purse.

The older woman patted her stomach. "Just a bit of reflux. I don't have the stomach for coffee anymore."

"Me either," Bixby said, as we said our goodbyes and left. "Magical flatulence has a way of destroying someone's appetite."

CHAPTER THIRTEEN

The streets were still dark the next morning when I drove to Whimsy. I'd slept no more than a couple of hours, and only that much because of the lava lamp in my childhood bedroom. Watching the blue blobs rise and fall had always soothed my nerves and put me to sleep.

"Dare I suggest upgrading to a bigger mattress?" Mr. Bixby said. "Better yet, a bigger bedroom. Your mother's dressing room has more square footage."

Mom had knocked down a wall between her room and the next to make a rather large walk-in closet. There was a cot for Sir Nigel in there, although he never used it. Instead, he took his rest from eternal rest on the couch downstairs watching *Survivor* re-runs. I didn't miss hearing that show on repeat while he was gone.

"I like my old room," I said, pulling up in front of my store. "It's cozy."

"That wicker armchair is barely big enough for a ragdoll, let alone a pedigreed dachshund. And I'm certainly not joining you on a skinny cot you outgrew by age eleven."

He wasn't wrong. But after years as a carnie sleeping in cars and tents, and then rolling among resorts, I was happy to be sleeping in the same bed night after night, no matter how skinny.

"That bed is surprisingly comfortable," I said, getting out of the car and reaching back for him.

"You mean comfort*ing*." He grunted as I hoisted him under one arm. "Just like I am. Your canine teddy bear."

"There's a bit of a groove in the middle, I suppose. But Mom kept my room just as I left it and she'd be insulted if I changed anything."

His grunt turned into a grumble as I closed the door and set him down on the sidewalk. "Mothers and daughters. I'm not equipped to understand that dynamic. I'll simply point out the house is huge and even with Ren and Sinda staying, there's room for you to branch out."

I smiled down at him as I stuck the key in the lock. "That reminds me of what Mom said when I asked if I was too old to play with dolls: 'you'll know when the time is right to stop because you won't enjoy it anymore.' That's how I feel about my old bedroom, Bixby. It still feels right."

Sniffling, he pretended to wipe away a tear with a beefy forepaw. "What a touching moment. Remind me to remind *you* about it next time you throw your mom to the proverbial wolves. She hit it right sometimes."

"I guess. Before magic became an issue, she mostly did okay."

The dog walked ahead of me into Whimsy and I locked the door behind us. "And when did magic become an issue?" he asked. "I already know the basics from my tour of your memories, but it would be interesting to hear your current spin on things."

Dropping my purse on the counter, I responded to his signal to set him beside it. This dog had trained me well in a few short weeks. Sometimes I felt like the pet performing on cue.

"Puberty," I said, simply. "That's when magic gets most of us."

"Maybe I don't want to hear it after all." He let his legs splay out and sank to his belly. "No wonder it's all laced up in drama."

The emotional ball was rolling down memory lane, however, so I turned on the lights and continued. "Probably would have helped if we'd realized what was happening at the time. I was in sixth grade when random things started happening around the house."

He crossed his front paws, proving he was more interested than he let on. "Like what?"

"Electrical outages, mainly. Circuits tripping. Bulbs exploding." I opened the blinds just a crack and stared into the still-dark street. "One day Mom got quite a shock when she turned on the kitchen light. I mean, literally. It was moments after she'd withdrawn my TV privileges for dropping a swear word. That's when she made the connection. Of course, I blamed Boz but electrical surges weren't his style, if he was even capable."

"It was your style? Sparky one, were you?"

"I'd like to say no but you've toured the facility." I tapped my temple. "Jilly and I spent so much time together as kids and she was always the cool-headed one. I thought she was smarter and nicer than me. And Gran's favorite, to boot. Now I see she was just older and more mature. And, well..."

"Not sparky."

"Exactly. Gran always doled out the same size portions to each of us, whether it was peas or candy. And when Jilly and I visited her together at the Briars earlier this year, that's what she did with her love, too. There was enough to go around then and now."

"Total waste of jealousy?" Bixby asked.

I nodded. "Since then I've wondered if that's behind how my powers manifested. Maybe I'd have developed less combustible techniques if I'd felt more comfortable in my skin. Once Mom realized what was happening to the circuits, she freaked out."

He chuckled. "Well, it is an old house. Could have gone up in a puff of smoke, taking the butler along for a ride."

I laughed, too, but my hand went to my chest as I remembered how it had felt to lose Mom's trust. She thought I'd blow up the house, the playground and maybe even my friends. "It wasn't my fault," I said. "It just happened."

"She knows that. I bet she thought it was *her* fault, either through nature or nurture. We've already established she had her hands full as the only magical person in the family. You, Bridie, and Jilly's clan all needed protection. And then along came young sparky."

"When you put it that way, I suppose it's no wonder she got so heavy-handed. She knew about my psychic abilities earlier, but the firepower took her by surprise."

"Unprecedented," he said. "It's the word of the week."

I picked up a cloth and started buffing the bare shelves. "I guess. We don't really talk about it."

"No one else in the family has stunning power? Your father, perhaps? There must be such a creature, although he's never mentioned."

"Never is right. You already know what I know about him. If you manage to pick up more from Mom, I'd be keen to hear it."

Splaying his toes, he examined his claws. "I'm not your spy. Unless there's something in it for me, of course."

"A pedicure? That could be arranged."

He tucked his paw under his chest quickly. "I don't like strangers manhandling me. Or even you, for that matter. So, no deal on the espionage."

"Suit yourself. I'm not that interested or I'd have asked Gran. Trust me, she'd like to tell her side of that story. I think it was a tale of forbidden love."

"Makes sense. All those fiery feelings came out in the offspring. The stuff movies are made of. I could do a voiceover."

"You have the pipes," I said, smiling as I put some effort into my polishing. Next week these shelves would get company and first impressions were critical.

He cocked his head, waiting. "So, what happened after you nearly electrocuted your mother in a fit of tween angst?"

"She sent Boz out into the world after me. That's when he got his talisman. You can imagine having a Victorian butler show up in your classroom might cause a little tension."

Bixby rolled onto one side and stretched out. He liked the smooth oak counter and knew he looked good on it. "Far be it from me to defend Sir Windbag, but he was just following orders. And Shelley was just trying to keep you from blowing the town up. She could have communicated better about it, no question. But emoting isn't her strong suit. Even a dog can see that."

I got up again and walked over to prop my elbows on the counter. The new store lights had been adjusted so perfectly to showcase the dachshund that I wondered if Bixby had given direct orders to the contractor. "Instead of bringing it up, I drove my powers underground. They felt bad and wrong. Illicit."

"And then, like all repressed feelings, they busted out in dysfunctional ways."

"Driving me out of town, as you know. No one in Wyldwood trusts me. They still think I killed Reggie Corby because we can't divulge the real culprit."

"That's not a worry for today," he said, jumping to his feet so suddenly my elbows gave out and my chin nearly hit the counter. "Clear, your mind must be, if you are to discover the real villains behind this plot."

When Bixby quoted Yoda, I paid attention. "What's wrong?"

There was a swirl of air on the window seat that rattled the blinds and then Harold appeared. The ghost dog's ears were flat and his hackles raised. If he had a tail, it would have stiffened like a bottle brush.

"Ask the furry cyclone," Bixby said.

I walked over to the window and did just that. "Harold, what's wrong?"

The answer became obvious as I peeked through the blinds again. I tried to swallow my gasp and failed.

Officer Slick frequently leaned against the lamppost or perched on the cement planter. Today, however, he was staring right in the window. We were separated only by a pane of glass and an irate ghost sheepdog. I could almost smell the man's breath.

"Sulphur," Bixby said. "Fermented grass. Roadkill. In this case, maybe a couple of carcasses roasting in the sunshine."

My fingers twitched to cover my nose but I wouldn't give the man the satisfaction. Instead, I flicked them at him to move along. Today I was an aspiring shopkeeper, imagining a time when people would come in to buy gifts for their nearest and dearest. If this surveillance kept up after opening, Officer Slick's presence would chase business away. Perhaps that was Oscar's plan. To drive me to bankruptcy since he hadn't succeeded in intimidating me out of the store.

A warm feeling replaced my irritation and I knew before seeing him that Drew Gillock was headed our way. He glanced in at me and then spoke to Officer Slick. Oscar's henchman took his time about leaving, and ran a hand over hair that felt greasy in my imagination. Only when he was near the corner did Harold stand down. The dog glanced back at me and then passed directly through the window and followed the man.

I didn't need to be a psychic to know the tension had just escalated.

"My job isn't to agree with you," Bixby said. "I like being the contrarian. But this time I actually think you're right."

CHAPTER FOURTEEN

I unlocked the door and the little bell overhead gave a flirtatious tinkle as Drew came in. The doorbell had been charmed before my time. Normally I wasn't a fan of antiques, but Ren and Sinda had found it at a stall in the weekly farmer's market and there was no denying it suited Whimsy beautifully.

"Isn't he just a ray of sunshine?" Bixby said, sweeping his long nose as a signal for me to collect him from the counter. The dog only truly enjoyed being carried when he could form a fur barrier between Drew and me. "It's for your own good. And I take back what I said about the single bed earlier. It sends exactly the right message to the universe. You're on the planet to work, not rest."

"Just keep quiet," I said, speaking aloud by mistake. I hadn't seen much of Drew lately and was both nervous and out of practice at juggling my magical impediments.

"Impediment!" Bixby was indignant enough to snap at Drew's sleeve. "You know you'll regret that, Miss Brighton."

"Good morning to you, too," Drew said, jerking his arm away from the dog. The chief looked slightly miffed, but it wasn't easy for me to get a good fix on his feelings. He was trained to conceal them, for starters. On top of that, he typically avoided meeting my eyes. Ivy Galloway said I transfixed him, like a mythical creature. A siren.

"A gorgon," the dog corrected. "Like Medusa, with the wild hair, who turned people to stone. Remember?"

I pressed my lips together, reminding myself to ignore the dog's taunts.

"Sorry, Chief Gillock," I said. "Seeing Oscar's sidekick outside always unsettles me. I was afraid I'd babble. And here I am, doing just that."

"And so you are," Bixby said. "Destined for a twin bed forever."

I squeezed the dog until he wheezed.

"Seems like you have a love-hate relationship with that dog," Drew said. "You're attached at the hip, literally, but he's always making sassy remarks." He grinned at me. "At least, that's how it sounds to an outsider."

"The doorbell thinks you're an insider," Bixby said. "Ooh la la."

"He is sassy," I said, setting the dog on the floor. Bixby refused to lower his landing gear and rolled onto his back instead. The very fact he exposed his belly to Drew told me the chief was eminently trustworthy. I'd barely seen those tiny tan spots, like dozens of dog freckles. "But I was glad to have a dog shield instead of just glass between me and Oscar's man. What did you say to get him to move on?"

"Threatened him with loitering. He's not a real cop, despite his uniform. Oscar seems to have him on the payroll, which means he's a glorified bodyguard."

He wasn't, though. There were more of those men. More of those uniforms. This one was just assigned to Oscar, and he probably wasn't alone. Mom always said for every uniform you saw there were two cops in plain clothes.

"Well, thank you for that. What brings you here so early?"

"Saw your lights and decided to take a look. I was on my way back to the crime scene."

"The Beanstalk?" I asked. "So, it's officially a crime scene now?"

He frowned. "Looks that way. Experts are still examining the espresso machine but it appears to have been rigged."

I went back around the counter. Drew had a gravitational pull like the sun and it was best to have something substantial between us. I couldn't afford to collide at random with a visiting chief of police. Not when there was so much debris in my own gravitational field. He was likely to get conked in the head with an Oscar-shaped meteor.

"How hard would it be to do that?" I asked.

"Not as hard as it should be." He rolled his dark eyes. "There's a how-to online for everything if you know where to look."

"Mitzy had detractors," I said. "I hope you're not including Renata and me among them."

He came over and despite the oak counter between us, I felt the warmth of his feelings toward me. As usual, I wished I could do something about them. He was the only man in my rather storied romantic career that had made me feel this way.

"Atwitter," Bixby said, still lolling on his back. "Like the sparky schoolgirl who blew things up with a hissy fit. Before she got a lava lamp to calm her down." He directed an eye at me. "Does Big Red know about the lava lamp? He probably should because it's very revealing."

Happily, Drew couldn't understand any of that, although he turned back to the dog curiously. "I don't believe you had anything to do with what happened to Mitzy," he said. "But Officer Barrow thinks otherwise. He's suggesting Ren was either addressing an old grudge or getting rid of future competition. Chief Dredger isn't convinced, either. The obvious choice is rarely the right one."

"Ren could never do something like that," I said. "Besides, she was scared of the espresso machine at the Beanstalk and hasn't learned to operate her own. I'm sure her former colleagues will confirm that. Ronna Tweeze and Mike Spenser, for starters."

He rested his hands on the counter. There was a white scar running across the left one, and I wondered if he'd been slashed with a knife.

"I'm not sure I can trust their stories," he said. "Because someone got to them first."

A little heat rose from my chest and I was glad to be wearing another one of Mom's frumpy dresses. There was never so much as a scooped neckline to give a blush away.

"Sorry. Yeah. I did have a brief chat with them. My best friend's honor is at stake, Chief. And perhaps more."

"That's exactly why you need to leave this in professional hands," he said. "For your safety... and hers."

I stared down at the scar on his hand and wished I could touch it. The sinewy tissue would likely tell me exactly how it had been sustained. Since Drew had defenses and didn't wear jewelry of any kind, getting a deeper look at his character would be difficult.

"Leave the man of mystery alone," Bixby said, righting himself and strolling over. "Let him do his job. You've got other priorities."

"I was just trying to speed things along," I told Drew. "Ren wants to open soon and it wouldn't be tasteful if a cloud is still hanging over the Beanstalk."

"Speaking of clouds... can you explain why you and Ren were covered in ash yesterday?"

"It was just dust," I said. "You know they're ripping her place up. In fact, I hear noise next door now. Let's go over and you can see for yourself."

His eyes narrowed, but he gestured for me to lead the way. "I bet if I took a sample of that so-called dust, I'd find ash."

I shrugged as I opened the door. "If you have time to chase red herrings, go ahead. There's a surprise waiting around every corner in this town."

And in every doorway, because as Drew walked out, a certain dachshund made a point of tripping him.

"Bixby, stop that," I said, as the dog tried to repeat the maneuver in Ren's doorway. "Someone's going to get hurt."

"I can take a kick or two to make a point," Bixby said. "Besides, I can vanish in the blink of an eye if I want."

The dog was still exploring the nuances of that ability. Once he accidentally disappeared while I was carrying him, which embarrassed both of us. I was left holding an invisible handbag till he returned, scared that if I moved my arm, he'd fall and break his leg or hurt his back.

Renata looked up at us and smiled as we came in. "Perfect timing. I wanted to give this espresso machine a try so that I could surprise Janelle with caffeine. But I can't make it work."

"Don't look at me," Drew said. "Cops live on instant coffee half the time."

"Just leave it for now, Ren," I said. "Let's get Norm Jenkins to come back for a proper demo."

"Not today," Drew said. "He's a suspect in Mitzy's death, too."

The color left Ren's rosy cheeks, likely over the word "too." I felt uneasy as well, but attributed the feeling to the visit from Oscar's henchman.

"Have you spoken to Norm yet?" Ren asked. "He hasn't returned our texts and he's usually so responsive."

Drew shook his head. "I'll drop by later, but he's lower on my list. The camera at the Beanstalk was out, but witnesses suggested he arrived after the others. Mitzy may have already passed away by then. Still, he may have seen something."

There was a tap on the glass and the door opened. It was Diggory Waring, the representative of Rare Earth fair trade coffee. He looked a little tired, and less cheery than when he'd visited the day before. "Good morning, folks. You open?"

"Not officially, of course," Ren said. "But you can join us, Diggory."

He walked straight up to the new counter and offered Ren a

large paper bag. "I brought you samples of a new line we're bringing in. You'd be the first in North America to serve these beans. It makes a memorable coffee—bold, yet velvety and lush. There are sweet notes of caramel and molasses with a hint of hickory. Let's do a taste test."

Ren's delicate eyebrows rose and then she shook her head. "Now isn't the best time, Diggs. Even if I could get the machine to work."

"There's never been a better time for a good cup of coffee," he said, pushing the bag toward her.

I stepped forward to help Ren. "Mitzy's situation hasn't been resolved, Diggs. Testing a new coffee would be—"

"Indelicate," Mr. Bixby said.

"Tacky," Bijou added. "Tick-tock tacky, Beans Buddy. Hit the road."

Ren pressed her lips together. I had far more experience blocking out voices and impressions but we were both utter newbies when it came to the dogs. It was tough to keep a straight face and grinning would be tackier than trying a new coffee.

"Disrespectful," I finished.

"That's right," Ren said. "I don't want to think about coffee until the case is resolved."

Diggs Waring shrugged. "Understood, but Mitzy probably wouldn't hold back if the shoe was on the other foot. She said some nasty things yesterday when we left here."

"Mr. Waring," Drew said. "That's unnecessary."

"Sorry, Chief. Just don't want Renata to feel bad about what happened."

Ren pushed the bag back across the counter. "I do feel terrible about Mitzy. We worked together for ages, and no matter what she said in the heat of a misunderstanding, I wished her nothing but the best."

Diggs' smile became a little sheepish. "Look, I hear you. I

supplied the Beanstalk for years and Mitzy always paid on time. But no matter how we feel, she's passed. The show must go on for Wyldwood's coffee lovers. Right now, you're the show, Renata."

A shiver ran through my best friend at the suggestion of profiting from someone's demise. "I won't open this place till Mitzy is properly put to rest. Perhaps we can talk about these beans another time."

"There's no time like the present. Like I said, you can be the first in North America to serve this new line." Ren had continued to push the bag until it was about to topple and Diggs grabbed it. "You're being shortsighted and that won't help you succeed in business in this town."

"Maybe not, but it'll make me feel like a decent human being," Ren said. "That's more important to me than business."

Diggs Waring opened a bag of ground beans. The scent billowed out and filled the store. I tried to pick up hints of caramel but there was nothing particularly refined about my nose. Regardless, the coffee smelled good. Mouth wateringly good.

"Just let me make you ladies a nice brew," he said. "You're stressed, and for good reason. What happened to Mitzy could happen to others."

I stared at the man, whose pleasant smile was firmly in place. "What is that supposed to mean?"

Mr. Bixby walked over to Drew, pressed a paw on his boot and yelled up, "Is chivalry dead, Big Red?"

Drew looked at the dog and blinked a few times. The chief seemed lost in thought, and I wondered briefly if he'd been affected by the memory spell at the Beanstalk, too. "I think the ladies would like you to go, Mr. Waring."

"Yeah, scram, Beanie Boy," Bijou said.

"But I can show you how to use this machine." Diggs resisted Bijou's encouragement to vacate. "You'll need to get comfortable with it."

Bixby joined Bijou in evicting the coffee rep. At the door, Diggs turned with his back to the glass, ignoring the dogs' aggravated barking. I couldn't help thinking of Harold and wishing he could create a targeted tornado to send this guy to the South American organic farms he represented. It was possible to do good work without being a very good person, it seemed.

Walking over, I waved the dogs away and pulled open the door for Diggs Waring. His arm brushed against mine and the scent of coffee enveloped me, inside and out. But for all his pushiness, I didn't detect a whiff of true malice against Mitzy. He was trying to make a buck off the situation, but that didn't make him evil.

Finally he stepped through the door and Bixby disappeared after him. Quite literally. Once my dog was outside, he vanished. Then Diggs Waring jumped, probably as an invisible set of teeth targeted his pant cuff at dachshund level.

I held the door open so that Bixby didn't walk right through it and startle Drew by reappearing. After a few moments, the dog strolled back in looking quite smug.

"I'm so glad he's gone," Ren said. "There's no way I'll do business with Rare Earth after all this."

Catching Drew's eye, I noticed he still seemed distracted. "You checked out Diggory Waring, right?" I asked. "When they left here yesterday he was arguing with Mitzy, remember?"

The chief nodded. Then he pulled out his notepad and flipped through it. "Plausible alibi," he said. "Credible witnesses, too."

"Well, he may be innocent of murder but he's guilty of poor judgement," I said.

Ren came around the counter to give Bijou a pat. "Crimes against decorum, at the very least. I'll happily serve instant coffee before I brew his new special blend."

The dog wriggled under her hand and recited, "Hickory dickory dock. The mouse ran up the clock."

Mr. Bixby rolled expressive eyes at me. "The ghost wind machine is looking better. At least he doesn't utter such inanities."

Drew put his notepad away and walked to the door. "I feel like I've missed a few beats here. Maybe it's time to find that instant coffee."

"Good luck with the case," I said, seeing him out. I let him brush my arm, too, noticing that the liquid sunshine he usually exuded had dimmed considerably. This was the chief fixated on a case, I supposed. No time for flirty rays.

Bixby waited till Drew was well out of earshot before chuckling. "Big Red makes you happy twice. Happy to see him come, happy to see him go."

I scooped the dog up and beckoned to Ren. "If we move fast, we might just manage to find a good cup of coffee before the chief does."

CHAPTER FIFTEEN

I glanced at Ren in the passenger seat as we drove out of town. "Did Drew seem a little distracted to you today?"

"Hearing about your lava lamp probably turned him off," Mr. Bixby said, lolling in Ren's lap while Bijou stretched out in the back seat. "Down at the Briars, he got this idea you were sophisticated. Someone had to give him a reality check."

"You still have the lava lamp?" Ren asked. "I loved that thing."

"It belonged to Gran, the hippie. Watching it reminds me of her. Very soothing."

Bixby pretended to doze off. I knew it was fake because he rarely slept and was perpetually full of energy. When I managed to catch some well-earned sleep, he probably stared at me all night.

He cracked one eye open. "You really think you're that interesting? My own memories keep me well entertained." Lifting a paw, he blocked my next comment. "And I mean my life *before* being stranded lifeless in Sinda's jewelry store. It was something else, I tell you. And yet I won't tell you."

Ren shook her head. "Did Drew actually hear you talking about the lava lamp, Mr. Bixby?"

"Maybe," the dog said. "He did seem a little dazed and I wondered if he'd finally tuned into my charm and wit."

I pressed the pedal down and Elsa rose to the challenge. "Drew didn't seem that off in Whimsy, but when we came over to your side, it got worse. Made me wonder if he got a hit of that enchantment at the Beanstalk. He wasn't exactly forthcoming, today. I wanted to touch him and find out what he knows."

"Touching the chief of police is a bad idea," Bixby said. "In my opinion. That's why I wanted him to know about the lava lamp and your twin bed. No point getting his hopes up."

Ren finally laughed, which may have been the dog's true goal. He had a soft spot for Ren and was probably feeling displaced by Bijou.

The fact that Bixby didn't give me sassy backtalk pretty much confirmed it, and I reached out to stroke his ears.

"Drew seemed fine to me," Ren said. "But I'm not the best judge of men. I thought Ethan might be interested in me but he hasn't asked me out."

"We're all busy doing the same thing... getting ready to launch new businesses. I expect you'll be the first one he invites to opening night."

She stared out the window, stroking Bixby's back. "We'll see. I thought about asking him to help with the espresso machine but didn't want to look too needy."

"That's exactly what we'll do if plan A doesn't work out," I said. "I'm sure Ethan will be glad to lend a hand, but we've got to check on Norm. It's so strange that he isn't answering and given what happened yesterday, I want to see with my own eyes that he's okay."

When we pulled up to a small, well-maintained house about 10 miles outside of Wyldwood, I was surprised to see Norm Jenkins lounging in a red Adirondack chair on the front lawn. It was a bit cool for chillaxing in the yard. Then I noticed a shovel, a bag of soil and a heap of bulbs. Getting his tulips planted was clearly a priority but it seemed strange that Norm hadn't responded to an espresso SOS. The phone was resting on the broad arm of the chair, so he couldn't have missed our calls and texts.

"Hello, girls," he said, as we got out of the car. "Beautiful day."

It wasn't, particularly. Enough clouds had gathered to remind me that winter was lying in wait for us. Wyldwood generally wasn't hit too hard, at least compared to towns further up the hill country range, but I still wasn't looking forward to bitter weather. I'd always chosen to find a new job further south at this time of year and didn't even own winter gear.

Norm crossed his leg at the knee and raised a mug to salute us. He hadn't seemed the type of guy to call us "girls." For an older man, he was pretty savvy. Not that I found it offensive. It wasn't something to file in the lexicon of forbidden words.

"Hey, Norm," I said, walking over with Bixby under my arm. "How are you doing?"

"Never better. Just enjoying a cup of java before I plant some bulbs. Who doesn't love a spring garden? But you've really got to plan ahead."

When I was beside him, I saw there was nothing in his mug. The white china interior was pristine. Nonetheless, he raised the cup to his lips and took a long, noisy sip.

"Uh-oh," Bixby said. "I thought I caught a whiff of you-know-what as we got out of the car. Norman got his brains addled and now he's drinking air."

"I do love a spring garden," Ren said. "But I've been calling you, Norm. We both have."

He picked up the phone and stared at it. "Which one are you? There's a lot of girls' names here. Janelle, Renata, Matilda and Ronna. They're all running together today because my mind's full of bulbs."

His mind was full of more than bulbs. The driveway and lawn were strewn with tools, ladders and even a snow blower now in pieces. It looked like he'd started a few projects and abandoned them.

"I'm Renata, and you installed an espresso machine for me yesterday. I guess I wasn't paying enough attention because I've already forgotten how to use it."

He offered a gentle smile. "Forgetting must be in the air, because I can't recall installing your machine." The twinkle that was so noticeable in his eyes yesterday had faded. "Or any machine for that matter. Is it something I do often?"

"Oh yes, you're a pro," I said. "Best in the business. We talked a few times and then I hired you to help Renata. I'm Janelle, by the way."

"That name does ring a bell." He set his cup in the grass and shifted uneasily. "But if we'd met, surely I'd remember." The twinkle flickered up for a second. "You're memorable girls."

I bent to put Mr. Bixby down and he started to poke around. Bijou was on a leash, although it wasn't needed. Ren was still worried about losing her, but the dog was so worried about losing Ren it would never happen.

Confusion and fear mixed on Renata's face now. "That's kind of you to say, Norm, and you were very gallant yesterday in defending me from my old boss. Do you remember that?"

He rubbed his forehead. "Not really, no. Is she one of the callers I listed?"

I caught his eye and shook my head. "I'm afraid she's passed away. Mitzy Lennox. She was one of your long-time clients."

"Mitzy, of course. Such a nice lady. Sounds like she had a bad day. Guess that's why she was grumpy."

Ren looked at me helplessly before forging on. "You followed Mitzy to try to smooth things over for me. Afterward, we couldn't reach you and got worried."

Gesturing around the lawn, he smiled again. "Nothing to fret about. I've just been busy."

"We can see that," I said. "Do you remember following Mitzy to the Beanstalk Café, Norm? I think that's where you may have lost your memory."

"A stroke, maybe?" he asked. "That would be a shame because it sounds like I was pretty good at my job. I guess I just retired." Patting the arm of the chair, he shrugged. "Time comes for all of us. Looks like I have plenty of hobbies to keep me busy."

Ren's dark eyes met mine over his white head and widened. Then she mouthed, "Do something."

I shrugged and mouthed back, "Like what?"

A certain dachshund strutted out of the garage saying, "Feels like the right time to use some of that magic you two talk about so much."

We didn't talk about magic enough, though.

"Maybe that's my point, if I have one," Bixby said. The dog wasn't concerned about speaking aloud, presumably because Norm was so caught up in confusion that he didn't register it. "You talk about stores and business and lava lamps and boys, when you should probably be talking about magic."

Ren pressed her lips together. It was harder for her to ignore his baiting than it was for me. I spent more time with him.

"Plus, we're twin flames," Bixby said. "Fated to be. Like that old song says... *If you try sometimes, you just might find... you get the dog you need*." He looked over at Bijou and sniffed. "The universe gets the order wrong sometimes."

"Shut up, wiener boy," Bijou said. "No time for jokes when Normie's lost his mind."

Had Norm lost his mind? It was entirely possible that someone had addled his thoughts just as I had those of the three people who'd tried to murder me. They were sitting in jail, whereas Norm was slumped in an Adirondack chair.

"Someone's stealing your signature move," Bixby said. "Doesn't that annoy you? It should."

It didn't annoy so much as alarm me. I hadn't even mastered my own ability and now someone had come along and one-upped me.

"And think about Big Red," Bixby added. "He's planning to visit Norm. What's he going to think when he finds him surrounded by bulbs and spouting gobbledygook?"

Drew was going to think I had a hand in it.

"Exactly. The only thing going for you is that you beat him to Norm." The dog tipped his head. "Plus, Big Red isn't firing on all cylinders himself today. That means you've got a chance to sort things out here. But don't dally."

I stared from Norm to Ren and back.

"Dallying," Bixby said. "Indecision is the sign of a weak mind. Just do something."

There was no way to know whether any interventions I might make would help or hinder. Norm was the first person I'd encountered whose thoughts were scattered even before I used my magic.

"So then it might have the opposite effect," Bixby said. "You won't know until you try."

I'd prefer to know in advance. Norm was a kind man who'd come to our defense yesterday and this was the thanks he got.

"He's not suffering," Bixby said. "On the contrary. Look at that smile."

It was a vacant smile. I doubted Norm had the capacity to hold the image of a tulip bulb in his head for longer than a second or two, before taking a sip of imaginary coffee.

"In other words, you're unlikely to do him any harm," Bixby said. "For goodness' sake, Renata, take a side. It's like you've both been stunned, too. Have you?"

My best friend shook her head.

"Harder," Bixby said.

This time we both shook our heads. We were stunned, but we hadn't *been* stunned. My thoughts were clear and Ren's eyes were sharp now, too.

"Do it, Witchy," Bijou said. "Work your woo-woo."

Fine. I squared my shoulders and amped up my comforting smile. "Norm, would you mind if I took a closer look at your ring?"

He stared at his left hand. "What ring?"

"The one on your other hand," I said. "It has an initial. And a little stone."

Offering his right hand, he shrugged. "Can't remember it. Maybe it came from my dad."

It was something he'd received in high school. An image came into my mind of a young man on a football field riding high in the arms of his team. They lowered him to the ground and someone offered a big trophy. The sound of cheering drowned out Mr. Bixby's wry commentary, which was actually a nice change.

It was a relief to find Norm was still in there. Other memories surfaced, of jobs, of a wedding, the birth of twin girls, and then, sadly, a funeral. As I pulled out this image, the old man winced and it slipped out of my mental fingertips. That was something he didn't want to remember.

Continuing to touch his ring, I tried to dabble closer to the surface in hopes of finding more recent memories.

Still, there was nothing at all relating to his espresso machine franchise. The only job I saw him doing was auto repair and he had a full head of dark hair back then. It was like his current life didn't exist.

Setting his hand back on the Adirondack chair, I said, "How are you feeling, Norm?"

His eyes met mine for the first time. "My head aches like someone's been clanging around in there with a socket wrench."

"Subtle, Janelle," Bixby said. "Got a plan B? I mean, other than calling Ethan and playing damsel in distress?"

"Yeah," I said, out loud this time. "You just hang tight, Norm. Help is on the way."

CHAPTER SIXTEEN

Mr. Bixby looked over at Bijou. "This is where it gets good. Hold onto your crumpets, poodle."

"Croissants," she said. "But I'm ready for whatever Witchy throws down."

He laughed, and even in my agitated state, I realized that was a first for these two remarkable dogs. Till now, they'd laughed *at* each other, not *with* each other.

"What are you going to try, Janny?" Ren asked.

Norm appeared entirely oblivious, but I decided to keep things vague. After all, someone had already stirred up his memories and they might come back for more.

"A little trick I tried on Boz," I said, waggling my eyebrows to remind her. I'd used a spell to retrieve a memory from our family ghost, and then hidden another one. There were several memory spells in my book and this was as good a reason as any to use them.

"Except for the fact you don't have the spell book with you," Bixby said, using our inside channel. "That isn't the kind of thing you just wing. Even the subtlest difference can blow off a door. Or fry a café owner."

I glared at him and shot back a silent response. "I did not fry Mitzy Lennox."

"Maybe someone's trying to make it look that way, though. Are you going to give them more to go on?"

"All I'm going to do is repeat a spell I've used to good effect before," I continued, still silently. What Norm couldn't hear, he couldn't repeat to anyone else. Unfortunately, it left Renata in the dark, too.

"Maybe we should have a chat with your mom," Ren said, getting the gist of it anyway. "It sounds like the kind of thing she was cautioning against."

"True," I said aloud. "But she meant new situations. I'm sure she'd be okay with the tried and true."

"You mean beginner's luck?" Bixby said, also aloud. "I wouldn't want to trust that."

Bijou rose to her full height so that she could look down on Bixby. "Why so negative, short stuff? Aren't we here to support and encourage our people?"

He sighed. "This *is* supporting my person. I'm the voice of reason when she's the voice of impulse."

"It'll be fine," I said. "I've got this."

"The last time you thought so you ended up covered in sunflower dust," Bixby said. He directed his muzzle up at Bijou. "Back off, brioche. This is what love looks like for us."

"Aw, sweet," I said, heading back to the car. "I love you, too, Bixby. And Ren and Bijou."

It was true, and my love for them meant I needed to do something—and fast. Our future was probably riding on it.

Elsa's trunk held a metal tackle box containing various ingredients used in common spells. At least, so I'd gleaned from the index at the back of *Everyday Spells for Everyday Magic*. I'd stocked up as much as I could, despite having opportunity for only a few experiments. What I needed for the memory spell was there, including an elusive berry I'd stolen from Maisie Gledhill's greenhouse.

I had never tried using a spell without saying it aloud, but I didn't want to leave a clue in Norm's mind for anyone coming afterward. Mom said each magical person's spell book was almost as unique as a fingerprint. If I remembered correctly, hers had small, bold lettering and black and white illustrations. Mine was more elaborate, with ornate and colorful drawings and a dry wit, at least in my opinion. I wondered who had owned it before it landed in my hands. We probably had something in common, although I wished the spells were more plainly worded.

"If they were, I reckon anyone could use it," Bixby said, joining me at the car. "You'd have people like Matilda and Spitz tossing spell bombs at random. Delivery's part of the package."

"I guess," I said. "Do you know if a spell works if you just say the words in your head?"

He scanned the lawn before answering. "I hate being your advisor on this. If it goes south, I wear it. I'm not a witch."

"Nor am I. We're something else. Something unprecedented. Right?"

"Yeah. We are that." After another long pause, he continued. "In my experience, people have implemented in silence. Just be very deliberate and very specific."

"Deliberate and specific," I repeated.

"Don't forget the 'very,'" he said. "Precision is essential, especially when altering thoughts someone's already altered. Get it?"

"Got it. I think." We walked back to the others, and when I offered Norm my hand, he took it with another vacant smile. If I did nothing but put a twinkle back in his eye, I'd feel as if I'd done some good.

"Aim higher," Bixby said. "Get something useful out of this."

I dropped the berry into a baggie with the other ingredients I'd taken from the tackle box, and closed my eyes. I thought hard about what I wanted to accomplish, and then chose another frequency to "say" the spell—one that even Bixby didn't understand. It wasn't that I didn't trust him, but if someone was hacking my skills, the less he knew, the better.

Norm looked down at my hand and his fingers tightened. "Audrey?"

Audrey was his wife. I had picked that up while touching his ring.

I swallowed hard and stayed quiet, hoping he wouldn't be traumatized by the memory.

"You overshot by a few years, Janelle," Bixby said. "Don't see any sign of a wife around here."

"Audrey," Norm said again. "I was scared, honey. You're the only one I'd admit it to, but it was like I was tethered. I couldn't get away from them."

I took a chance and asked, "What did they do, Norman?"

"They killed that woman, hon. You know the one. From the café. She made a good coffee but that's about all that was good about her. I just wanted her to calm down but someone else got to her first. She was yelling when I came in. I had a key but I shouldn't have used it. Walked right into a situation and there was no turning back."

"Who beat you there?" I asked. "To the Beanstalk?"

"That lady who used to do your hair, Audrey. She was outside, and the gal from the pet store. They didn't seem to recognize me and they didn't want to come in." Norm stirred uneasily. "Inside, there was a man. At least I think so because I started feeling kind of funny. Queasy, like after eating bad seafood. He came up behind me and put a hand on my shoulder. When I looked down I saw a ring with a red stone. Ruby, I guess. Like your birthstone."

I didn't need to ask about the ring. The serpents that began swirling in my inner landscape told me Oscar Knight had been at the café yesterday. He was very likely the one who'd tampered with Norm's thoughts and would certainly have the skills to do so.

"What did he want?" I asked, as gently as I could, given how hard my heart was pounding.

"He wanted me to forget what I saw."

"And did you?" I asked. "Forget everything?"

"Everything." A tremor passed over him. "Didn't have to ask me twice, Audrey. I wanted to forget it all."

"Norm, can you remember just a little bit? Like what he wanted from Mitzy?"

His whole body tensed but he spit out the word. "Money. She said she didn't have it. He said it was her last chance. And that it was time to do something about the girl, like she promised."

"What girl?" I asked, fearing he'd say Renata's name. My friend would be terrified.

Norm looked up at me and his eyes weren't vacant anymore. In that moment, at least, he knew he wasn't speaking to his dead wife. "You," he said. "I'm so sorry. But he wants you gone."

"Gone," I repeated. "Oscar Knight wants me gone."

Norm looked down and scraped his nails across the red paint on the arm of the chair. It chipped off in flecks that drifted on the cool breeze like dried blood. "I'm afraid so. And your mother. He said someone has to do it."

I tried to release Norm's hand but he wouldn't let go. For one awful moment, I worried Norm was the one Oscar had commissioned for the job of ridding the world of Janelle Brighton.

"Let go, Norman," I said. "You want to let me go."

He nodded. "I do. If you don't mind, it would be nice to stay here with Audrey for a bit. She always planted twice the bulbs we needed. Half for the squirrels, she said."

Once his fingers released their tight grip on my hand, I led the others back to the car.

"This is horrible," Ren said. "In so many ways. We can't leave Norm like that."

I turned the key and then spun Elsa back toward town. "No choice, Ren. I can't do more because Norm doesn't want to remember what happened. And if he did, he'd be at risk from Oscar. Right now, he's safest here making a mess."

"You'll ask your mom?" Ren said.

"I will, I promise. Unfortunately, it means she'll come home right away."

Mr. Bixby settled onto Ren's lap with Bijou, managing to shove the bigger poodle into the door. His attitude outweighed hers by far.

"Perfect," he said. "I've always enjoyed a good showdown."

CHAPTER SEVENTEEN

I dropped Ren and Bijou at the store for an appointment with a contractor and left them to brief Sinda about what happened. Then I turned Elsa around and drove the few blocks to the town's public services office.

"We could have walked," Bixby said. "I appreciate an opportunity to mark my turf."

I frowned at the light as it turned amber. "That's what you're worrying about? We just heard Oscar Knight has a target on my back."

"Nothing new there," he said. "Whereas there might be some pee-mail I haven't read. Discount me as you may but there's a lot of information on trees, poles and patches of otherwise mundane grass. Oscar's ridgeback gets around town, you know."

"Huh. I guess I never thought about it that way. Magical people love their pets, too."

"Even the flatulent ones," he said. "The humans, that is."

I stopped again at the next traffic light. They seemed to be aligned against me, today, but it was probably because I was filled with fresh urgency. "I'll take you on a good walk when we're done at City Hall."

"Do you have an appointment with the mayor you haven't told me about?"

I laughed and rolled forward as the light turned green. "Wyldwood's mayor isn't exactly folksy. Ruthann Longmuir has been in office for more than thirty years, yet I've never met her."

"Getting elected that many times in a town like this is quite a feat. She must have friends on both sides of the magical divide."

"Probably a delicate dance," I agreed, as I hit another amber light. "I sure wouldn't want that job."

"All you want to do is run your little store with Sinda downstairs and Ren next door," he said.

"That's right." I gunned it through the intersection. "A simple life."

"Which involves being alive. And keeping your nose clean."

I tapped my fingers on the steering wheel. "I catch your drift, and yes, I'll call Mom this evening. Contrary to what you might think, I actually want her to come home. I mean, I want to make sure Gran's safe, but now that I know Oscar is actively gunning for us and may even have hired a hitman—or hit-person—I do want some magical backing. We got lucky with him the first time, partly because of Bijou's intel."

"I hate to give the poodle credit, but it took him by surprise and that probably doesn't happen often."

Easing up on the gas, I took a few deep breaths. "I figured with Mom out of town he'd back off. Now it looks like Mitzy's death may have had something to do with me after all."

"But it probably wasn't your growth spell gone wrong. That must be a relief."

I cracked my window and then scowled as another light turned amber. "Well, I suppose. If there's any upside to this news, it's that I didn't fry Mitzy."

"And you did quite well with Norman," Bixby said. "Let's see the cup as half full."

Hitting the brakes, I sighed. "Whereas Norm's is quite empty at the moment. I need to circle back and help him when it's safe."

"Hopefully before winter turns him into a popsicle. I don't trust he'll go inside of his own accord."

"And hopefully before Oscar takes Mom and me out of commission. There are quite a few people with patchy memories about yesterday, but Norm took the worst hit."

The dog insinuated himself into my lap, which told me more about my state of mind than anything else. Bixby didn't splash comfort around. It was to be doled out only as strictly necessary.

"Why does he have such a bee in his bonnet about Shelley?" he asked, nudging my hand for a pat.

I responded to the hint and scratched his ears. "She won't say. At least, not yet."

"And your gran doesn't know?"

"Mom thinks it would put us at too much risk. Plus, she doesn't trust anyone—except Boswell, I presume."

With the dog on my lap, I was forced to roll the last few blocks more slowly. I couldn't risk squishing him against the steering wheel.

"There was a time all the Brightons got along, Bixby," I said. "Gran said so. It was back when her own mom was alive. They took pride in their clan. Those who were stronger looked after those who weren't."

"What happened?" he asked, prodding my hand again. "Because there are some big rifts now."

"I'm not even sure. It was before my time. Mom and Aunt Eva were already bickering when Jilly and I were kids." I ran my fingers along his sleek back. "I'd love to find a way to heal the rift someday. We'd be so much stronger as a team."

"A laudable goal, and you have my full support."

"In the meantime, I'll focus on building my new friend-family, with you, Sinda, Ren and Bijou. And Harold, if he's willing." I sighed as we hit yet another amber light. "Maybe Drew, if I'm lucky. The Brighton women mostly scare men away but Jilly seems to have broken that pattern with Asher Galloway."

"If romance is really what you want, you might make it work," he said, kicking at my dress to find a better position. "Jilly doesn't have the pesky problem of stunning people or melting things. It's so inconvenient. Imagine what a misfire could do to a twin bed?"

I didn't know whether to laugh or cry, so I chose laughter. "Plus my lava lamp. Since it's not real lava."

"That's the spirit," he said. "There will be plenty of time to ponder such things after we put Oscar Knight in his place. Again." He rested a chunky paw on my hand. "Don't doubt yourself for a second, Janelle. No matter what I say sometimes, I have full faith in you."

"I appreciate that, my friend. I don't doubt you for a second, either." I lifted my nose to the open window and released a little wish into the universe. It seemed impossible that my family would ever heal the rift. There was too much water under too many bridges. But that didn't stop me from wanting it just the same.

"You're willing to put your grudges fully behind you?" he asked. "The ones that kept you on the run nearly half your life?"

"Yeah. I guess I finally am." I eased him back into the passenger seat as we got closer to the municipal parking lot. "Do you think there's such a thing as therapy for families like ours?"

"Some enterprising shrink is probably making a killing. Possibly literally," Bixby said. "It has the makings of a fabulous reality show. But no one would believe it."

I pressed the gas to beat it through the last possible light and made it by a hair. It was the kind of move I'd only try when the police were preoccupied with other matters.

"Take that," I said, hanging a sharp turn into the parking lot.

A strange rumble from the passenger seat made me slow to a crawl and turn. What I saw made me gasp. I started to laugh and then stopped when I realized how much this would hurt my dog's pride.

Harold had joined Bixby and was trying to claim the seat. Since all the Aussie had at his disposal was wind, he was using it to good effect. Mr. Bixby had been blown into the corner against the door and his ears were flapping in a most undignified way.

"Easy, Harold," I said, wondering how long the ghost dog had been with us. I had the distinct impression he'd been eavesdropping on the conversation. "That looks like an abuse of wind power."

Mr. Bixby tried to weigh in but his words were blown right out of his mouth.

"Harold, stop that right now. It's good to see you, though. Did you pick up anything useful from Oscar's henchman?"

The ghost sheepdog ignored the question and put his paws on the dashboard. I hoped the dog wouldn't pull any pranks on Elsa. It wouldn't take much to send the poor old girl up in a vortex, never to be seen again.

"Indeed. The same could happen to your canine," Bixby said, struggling to his feet. "Perhaps I deserve the same consideration."

"He's right, Harold. Easy on Bixby, Elsa and my hair. I appreciate a breeze as much as the next gal but you never know who we might run into at City Hall."

I cracked my window more and Harold literally blew across my face and vanished through it as I maneuvered into a parking space.

"No denying I envy him that," Bixby said, licking his shoulders and chest to slick his fur. "Do you think he'll carry that skill over when you call him back to life?"

Turning off the car, I shrugged. "That's why we're here. To figure out where Harold once belonged. I don't know how to call him over without having someone he loves beside me. And yet, I figure he is part of this puzzle we're solving. Otherwise, why arrive the day Mitzy died?"

I pulled down the visor, checked my makeup and smoothed my hair. It was a stalling tactic, but this time Bixby let it go.

"Would you mind doing the same for me?" he asked, sliding back into my lap. "Next time I'll willingly take a back seat to the furry windmill."

"If only we knew when he'd arrive," I said. "He might have been helpful at Norm Jenkins' place but took off doing his own thing. I still haven't earned his trust, I guess."

"Maybe he's working for a different leader," Bixby said, turning to let me slick down his other side. "Bijou wanted to please. Maybe a little too much. Harold's got his own agenda. Hardly a pack mentality."

Letting that go, I got out of the car and carried Bixby through the parking lot and into the municipal offices attached to City Hall proper. The senior citizen behind the plexiglass shield at the information desk frowned when she saw us. "No dogs here, ma'am. On top of that, all dogs need to be leashed throughout Wyldwood."

I pulled a leash out of my pocket. It was studded with rhinestones, a gift from Sinda that we hadn't used. Clipping it to Bixby's collar, I checked the woman's name tag and gave her a hospitality smile. "This is my therapy dog, Mrs. Willard. I get claustrophobic, especially in old buildings like this one." I gave a shudder. "Gosh, it's starting already."

"Why old buildings in particular?" she said, taking the bait.

"Ghosts. You never know what might pop out and— Oh!"

Harold appeared behind the plexiglass and took a few rapid turns in the small space. Loose paper shot up, including several copies of the *Wyldwood Springs Star*.

The paper, along with a box of tissues, some badges and a most unfortunate African violet, whirled in a wide funnel. While the wind tugged at the old woman's eyeglasses and her floral scarf whipped in her face, I slid quickly past the security gate and into the records office. Once inside, the wind died down and I smoothed my curls and then Bixby's fur.

"He's annoying but useful," the dachshund said. "Now what?"

I had hoped the public records were, in fact, public. Instead, I found another senior guarding the castle. This time it was a gentleman.

Since Harold was still busy creating a storm in the foyer, I amped up the wattage on my smile and leaned over the man's desk to offer my hand. He took it, and I encouraged him mentally to let us go about our business.

"There's subtle and there's useless," Bixby said. "Push a little harder."

After what happened to Norm, I didn't want to risk meddling with this man's mind. Instead, I stuck with patience and persistence, chitchatting about the weather and the fall harvest fair while continuing to touch his arm long after he'd released my hand.

"How can I help you today?" he asked, at last. "Are you looking for public records?"

I nodded eagerly. "I found an old dog tag in my yard. Forgot to bring it today, silly me. But it looks like it dates back at least thirty years and I thought the family might like to have it. Do you track dog registrations that far back?"

"Oh, sure. We keep records of everything," he said, getting up from the desk. "How about I give you a hand? I'm a dog lover, too." He examined Mr. Bixby closely. "Especially dachshunds. They're a big breed in a compact package."

"A man of great discernment," Bixby said. "You may allow him to carry me."

As the old man accepted the dog, any remaining reservations he may have had faded away.

We sat down at a bank of computers, and with one hand, our host called up the name Harold in the town's past. There were dozens of hits—far more than I expected. It was the canine equivalent to John or Emma, it seemed. I urged him to refine the search by Australian shepherd and all the Harolds vanished from the screen. Replacing that with sheepdog brought six back, four with surnames and addresses.

"Wonderful," I said, taking the print-out he gave me, along with my dog.

"Would you like me to make some calls for you?" he asked. "Sometimes it's better coming from our offices."

"Even more wonderful if you can spare the time," I said.

His phone buzzed and he pulled it out of the pocket of his trousers. "You'll need to wait a few minutes, young lady. There's some kind of disturbance out in the vestibule. The mayor's come down."

"May I suggest a discreet exit?" Bixby said, as the old man hurried away.

I slipped out of the records room and merged into the growing crowd of staff and citizens. Mayor Longmuir stood among them, instantly recognizable despite her faded brown bob, tan blouse and slacks, and flat Mary-Janes. I sensed her look had been carefully curated to blend into the masses, which was unusual for someone in public office. Only during election season did Ruthann Longmuir bust out some color to attract the necessary votes.

Today, she surveyed the ongoing vortex in the foyer, glanced in my direction and then slipped out the side door to the parking lot.

I followed, watching as she got into a beige hybrid car and left in a hurry. Small-town mayors didn't usually get security details, but I figured she might in a place like Wyldwood. She would have friends and enemies, like any politician, but her enemies would have magic on their side.

"You've got to be kidding me," Bixby said, as I tossed him rather rudely across to the passenger seat and jumped behind the wheel. "We're tailing the mayor?"

"She wants us to," I said, racing after her.

"Whatever makes you say that?"

"Instinct. Plus all the lights are green."

"They were all amber driving in. That's just how it works."

I shook my head and took a sharp right after the beige hybrid. "Ruthann caught my eye. Probably wants a one-on-one out of the spotlight."

He dug his claws into Elsa's worn upholstery to brace himself. "You've never met her before. Why you? And why today?"

"Very good questions," I said. "They'll be the first ones I ask. If I can catch her."

CHAPTER EIGHTEEN

Ruthann Longmuir lost me long before reaching Withrow Park, but I knew where she was going. Not because of my psychic abilities, or even Bixby's sharp nose, but because that's where I went when I didn't want to risk being seen or overheard. There were so many pretty parks closer to the town's core that few made it out this way. I'd always wondered why the parks department seemed to invest a little more in the shiny white pebbles that lined the paths, the wrought iron fences that blocked off the waterfalls, and the oak benches with bronze trim that never tarnished. Now I knew the mayor shared my favorite getaway.

I set Bixby on the ground and slipped his leash over my wrist. "Let's play pretend, Bixby. I'll pretend I'm a normal shopkeeper and you pretend you're a regular dachshund. Here we are in a beautiful park taking a walk."

"Fine, got it," he said. "No chitchat."

"And no strange stunts, please. I remember what you did to Chief Gillock when we were here last time."

"I cocked a leg but nary a drop was spilt," he said. "We've already established that I need a full tank to make my rounds in town. The mayor's sensible shoes are safe."

"That's it. No more witticisms. Do not make me laugh."

"Your choice." He trotted ahead of me at the end of the lead. "Suddenly the world is a vale of tears."

Following him, I sighed. The more I tried to suppress his voice, the more he burst out in other ways unbecoming of a pedigreed dachshund.

A few words drifted back. "Says who? When you pen your etiquette book for formerly deceased dachshunds, I'll expect a signed copy. Gratis. For services rendered."

He simmered down by the time we neared the mayor, who was standing in front of the tallest falls. Her fine hair had flattened against her head from the mist, whereas mine increased in volume with every step. I wanted to whip out the silk scarf I'd put in my purse for just such occasions but was worried I'd look like I was trying too hard.

"You are trying too hard," Bixby said. "Otherwise you wouldn't have chased the mayor like Janelle Bond of old."

"Quiet," I said before summoning my very best smile. "Why hello, Mayor Longmuir. Nice to see you."

"You handle that old heap well," she said, turning to scan me with hazel eyes that verged on brown and matched her neutral palette.

"That's my Elsa," I said. "And you handle your hybrid like a Maserati." I offered my hand and she ignored it. "I'm Janelle Brighton. I don't believe we've met."

Her lip twitched up on one side. "Sure, we have. Once upon a time you and Jilly Blackwood were the prettiest girls in all of hill country."

"Still are," I said, folding both hands over the rhinestone leash. "We're aging like fine—"

"Witches," she said. "Your mom looks a little younger every year."

I thought about how to answer that and decided to take the high road. "No one likes that word, Mayor, and it really doesn't suit Jilly at all. Still, she looks gorgeous."

"No argument there. I saw photos when she was down from Clover Grove last month."

My hospitality mask wasn't securely anchored in place and now it dropped right off. "Photos? What photos?"

"Security. Obviously." She turned to stare back toward the parking lot. "It was big news when you came home. Not reportable news, but news all the same. I was fully briefed."

"Briefed? On my homecoming? Why?"

"That's a lot of question marks for someone known for her poise."

"Who says I'm known for my poise?"

"You?" She shot a question mark back and lifted one eyebrow.

I granted her the first point. "You're right. I said that when I worked in hospitality. My poise has taken quite a hit here."

"Temporary, I'm sure. You know how to handle yourself. If my source is to be believed, you put Oscar Knight in his place."

"Who said that?" I asked, more shocked still. "The town gossips?"

"Not unless you include Oscar among them."

The leash fell out of my hands and Mr. Bixby elected to park on my shoes, perhaps to ground me. I was just as glad he was hiding Mom's footwear. The mayor's brown leather flats suggested she didn't care about such things, but I still did. "Oscar Knight said I put him in his place?"

"Not in so many words, but I read between the lines." This time she really did smile, which made her look much younger and somewhat elfin. It made me wonder if she had more powers than the typical mayor.

"All I wanted to do was rent that retail space and run a gift store," I said. "Oscar tried to trip me at every turn."

"That's his way. We've known each other a long time. Main Street is his playground."

As her smile expanded, mine shrank. Mom must have been right about Ruthann's relationship with Oscar Knight. "You two are friends."

"Not exactly. But I know his vulnerabilities and he knows mine. It takes some fancy footwork sometimes but we keep the peace."

"Well, I may have put Oscar in his place but he isn't staying there," I said. "I have that on good authority."

"Hard to keep a man like him down," she said. "For long, anyway. And word to the wise, Janelle... there are few good authorities here."

I wanted to pace but the dog sitting on my shoes forced me to stand still. So I settled for crossing my arms. "Is that why you wanted to meet today? To warn me about Oscar's vendetta?"

She shook her head. "I came down to say hello when I saw you on my security feed. But then your personal cyclone started stirring things up and I thought we should speak more privately."

"I have no control over the wind, Mayor. Really."

"I suggest you gain control over that particular wind, Janelle, and quickly. I refuse to have that sort of thing happening in municipal buildings. Why were you even there? Surely your new store and the business with Mitzy Lennox are distraction enough without digging around in public records."

I noticed her eyes looked more green than brown now. She really was a chameleon. "There's a stray dog at the manor. A tricolor Australian shepherd with a tag that says Harold. I'm trying to find out where he belongs."

"That's what Animal Services is for. I'm a pet lover, so I make sure they're well-funded."

"Glad to hear that, but when an animal shows up at my place, I'm duty bound to find its owner." I didn't drop my eyes. "Are you aware of anyone missing a dog fitting that description?"

"All those sheepdogs run together for me," she said, turning away a little too quickly.

Reaching out, I caught her wrist. "Mayor, this sheepdog is really important to me. I get so invested in my rescues, you see." With my free hand, I pointed down to the perfectly poised dachshund. "Mr. Bixby was my first. He's changed my life."

The dog tipped his head one way and then the other. He only did the double head tilt when he was really pouring it on. Apparently the mayor was of sufficient stature to warrant it.

I started to tell her about finding him in Sinda's jewelry store down south as a cover for trying to read her mind. Unfortunately, I hadn't really mastered multitasking while mindreading yet. It took all my focus if I was looking for something so specific as a sheepdog in a haystack.

"Janelle," she said, while I was still working up a head of steam. "I know what you're doing."

"Babbling? I guess I'm a little intimidated by you."

She looked down at my hand and then pried my fingers off her wrist one by one. "Not too intimidated to try picking my pocket. I am aware when someone is rifling through my mental files. Your mom tried it, and other Brightons before her. It didn't work then and it won't work now."

"I'm sorry, Mayor. It was rude. I wasn't aware—"

"That others are aware of such things, evidently. Some training wouldn't go amiss if you plan to take on people like Oscar."

"But I don't," I said. "Plan to take on people like Oscar, that is."

"Well, you'll have a chance to work it all out when you're organizing the Christmas festival."

"Oh, brother," Bixby said, finally breaking his silence. "Must we?"

"Must we?" I repeated aloud to the mayor.

"It's not a command performance," she said. "But I really don't like tension in my town and nothing brings people together like

Christmas. Oscar's always on the committee, and very little changes. Fresh blood is exactly what we need."

Bixby let out a snort that made the mayor smile again. There was no need for translation.

"Oh, come on," she said. "I'm on the committee. Christmas is something I care deeply about and as a retailer, you will, too."

"I'm so busy, Mayor. Particularly this year with the store opening and my mom away."

"All the more reason, young lady. Where is your festive spirit?"

Bixby cleared his throat. "I'm sorry to say this, Janelle—well, not really—but *duh*. The mayor is offering to babysit you so Oscar doesn't wipe you off the map."

"Oh," I said. "You know, I've reconsidered, Mayor. I'd love to help bring Christmas to Wyldwood. I have plenty of fresh ideas."

"Wonderful! The first meeting is this afternoon in Tingle Square." She glanced down at the dog. "You deserve better than those shoes, Mr. Bixby."

"You're telling me, your highness." He snickered. "Of course, everyone's high compared to me."

"He seems like quite a character," the mayor said. "I have a cat just like him."

"I hate cats on principle," Bixby said. "Tell yours I said so."

The mayor smiled on cue, almost as if she understood him. "You can call me Ruthann, Mr. Bixby."

Did she understand him?

Her smile became enigmatic and she started walking away.

"Mayor Longmuir," I called after her, "you mentioned other Brightons."

She stopped suddenly. "Hush now. That's not the kind of thing you shout about, even under cover of a waterfall."

I walked over to her. "But you're talking about my family. And Mom's the only Brighton I know about who can—what did you call it? Rifle through file cabinets."

"I'm older than I look, Janelle. Your grandmother's cousin was inclined to… well, take liberties."

"Cousin Liberty?" I asked. "She's long gone now."

She started walking again and I followed. "Yes. It's really for the best that—"

Her last words were swallowed by a rising wind. Sticks and dust blew up and we all coughed.

"Mayor!" I called again. "Are you saying—"

A bit of dry grass clogged my throat and nearly choked me.

Harold was running after the mayor but she had some twisty choreography that was like a variation on Irish step dancing.

Finally he got ahead of her and forced her back, whirling until she spun to face me. Far from being afraid, she narrowed her eyes and frowned.

"I won't discuss this with you again, Janelle. Turn down the wind."

I flicked my fingers at Harold, wondering if he'd obey. He gave me a cheeky look and then raced off, tossing up a last eddy of dead leaves.

The mayor started walking again. This time she didn't turn and I don't even know if she spoke aloud, but I heard her words anyway: "Liberty had a sheepdog."

I started running, but she stayed well ahead of me. For a woman of about Gran's age, she was extremely fit.

"Mayor—" I tried once more.

"Don't follow me again," she called. "I'll have you arrested."

CHAPTER NINETEEN

Mr. Bixby laughed all the way back to town. "I like Ruthann. She's downright delightful. Don't you agree?"

"Hardly," I said. "She practically called me a hack."

"Well, if the shoe fits..." He chuckled again and stuck his nose out the window. "She's having you followed, by the way."

I glanced in the mirrors and saw nothing. "Followed! Why?"

"Probably to keep you safe. It seems like she's doing all she can to help without overtly antagonizing Oscar Knight."

"And she wants me to hold up my end by not overtly antagonizing Oscar."

He turned to glance at me. "Sounds fair. You can still antagonize him... just not overtly."

I laughed. "On the Christmas planning committee."

"Exactly. He's likely to be quite antagonized simply by having you there."

Slowing, I braked at the first intersection. The lights were all against us again, whereas the mayor had likely sailed through. "Going to a town meeting today is the last thing I want to be doing."

"Never too early to get into the Yuletide spirit. This will give you a chance to keep an eye on Oscar while the mayor keeps an eye on both of you. It's totally festive."

"But Norm Jenkins' memories suggest Oscar killed Mitzy, either directly or indirectly, and that he's really gunning for me. Even the mayor thinks I'm on Oscar's hitlist."

"Perhaps he'll show his hand as we're choosing Christmas carols. It's important to see the upside, here."

My usual spot in front of Whimsy was free, so I pulled in and turned off the car. "What do you make of what the mayor said about Liberty Brighton? Do you think Gran's cousin is alive?"

"I'm not the psychic. What do *you* think?"

I shrugged. "Ruthann knows how to cloak her thoughts. I didn't pick up a single thing when I touched her."

"Well, she certainly suggested Harold, the canine cyclone, belonged to this cousin. Perhaps he came to you with tidings of great joy. Or something else."

Nodding, I gathered my purse and Bixby. "Ghost dogs come into my life for a reason, it seems. I wonder if Harold wants to cross back to help Liberty. Gran assumed her cousin's been dead for decades. Perhaps Liberty's just been in hiding all these years."

"Another magical feud, like the one that drove your Mom into a bunker?"

"Possibly." I got out of the car and set the dog on the ground. "How about we take the walk I promised you while I think about what to do next?"

Bixby perked right up. "Sure! Sometimes the simple pleasures of being a dog restore me like nothing else. I have the feeling things are going to heat up around here."

"Me, too." We ambled down the street together and fell into a companionable silence. For a time, however brief, we were just a woman and her dog enjoying a walk on a fall day that had brightened considerably.

On the way back, his tail was up and his ears forward. "How

about I let you tell me your plan?" he asked. "Even though I've already reviewed it?"

"Feeling generous, are you?" I said, enjoying the cool air and pretty flower displays outside every store.

"That's what a walk will get you. You could try it more often."

"Okay, well, as you already seem to know, I was thinking about casting a spell to locate Liberty. There's got to be something in that book about revealing things."

He lifted his leg in front of the pet store and allocated his last drops on the planter. It was a good place to post his whereabouts since more than half the town's dogs visited.

"That seems a little obvious," he said. "Bridie suggested her cousin had impressive skills, and we know now she might have faked her own death. I doubt you can flush her out with an everyday spell from your everyday magic book. Liberty would probably deflect you easily."

"But Gran suggested Liberty was, well..."

"Crazy, yes. To the non-magical everyone probably looks that way. Even you."

"I suppose." Walking the last block, I continued to muse. "Think about what happened with Mom. She was poisoned and dragged herself off to hide. I thought she was crazy, when she was just sick from a bad case of magic." We reached Whimsy and I unlocked the door. "If Cousin Liberty's been sick or in hiding for thirty years, she really will be crazy now."

He trotted inside ahead of me. "Let's cross that bridge when we come to it. If we can't spell her out of hiding, what's Plan B? I didn't see one when I was poking around in your noggin."

"Can you add noggin to the forbidden lexicon? I don't like it."

"Nothing wrong with noggin. You'll need to make a better case for banning it."

I lifted him onto the counter and then texted Sinda and Ren, who came over from next door. After bringing them up to speed, I flipped through the spell book, lingering over one for revealing lost items.

"Cousin Liberty isn't a set of keys or eyeglasses," Bixby said. "If it were that easy, your mom would have tried it."

"Maybe she has tried it," Ren said. "Let's give her a call and find out."

"She's probably spying on us right now," I said, looking around. "Mom? You there? We know about the relative you never mention. In case you were wondering."

"I blocked her," Ren said. "In fact, I set up a better security feed for both stores. If your mom could hack in that easily, so could others."

"She might have more devious ways," I said, tapping a page. "Like this one: How to keep an eye on a distant prize."

"You're the prize, I take it?" Bixby said.

"Depends on the day, I suppose. I thought I was Mom's only living magical relative, but that turned out to be another lie. Nothing is ever as it seems here."

"As you expected when you chose to come home," he said. "But you found Ren. You found your missing mother. And you found that silly poodle, for better or worse."

He stared down at Bijou, who was leaning against Ren's shins, as usual. "Better better better," the poodle said. "Little Mister High and Flighty."

"Flighty? That's the pot calling the kettle black." Turning back to me, he said, "There's likely another way to find your relative. A more direct route."

Bixby swept his long nose toward the window seat, where Harold lounged in a moment of rare repose. The sheepdog's mouth hung open in what appeared to be a happy pant. Perhaps he was waiting for me to realize he was the clue.

"Harold," I said, walking over to him. "Did you belong to my gran's cousin, Liberty?"

His mouth closed and he turned his muzzle away.

"Let me rephrase that. Do you *currently* belong to Liberty Brighton?"

He swiveled in the other direction, refusing to meet my eyes.

I leaned over to check his tag for a serial number to match against my print-out from the records office, but any engraving had worn off during his not-so-eternal rest.

"Harold, come on," I pressed. "You're here for a reason. Either you came on your own to help Liberty or she sent you to get me. Either way, someone thinks I can help."

"Or someone thinks they can help you," Bixby pointed out.

I considered that. "Possible, as the mayor's taken an interest in keeping me alive, too. Ruthann Longmuir wanted me to know about Liberty, Harold, so I'd appreciate it if you could make the introductions."

"Ideally before we get into more trouble with spelling 101," Ren said. "We can't help Miss Brighton if we're in jail. And we might need her to keep us out."

Finally the Aussie met my eyes with what seemed like a calculating look. Had I passed the trust test, yet? If it was about magical ability, probably not. If it was about character, maybe.

I knelt beside him. "You probably heard what I said in the car earlier. About bringing the Brightons together. That's truly my goal because we'll be stronger as a united front. It all starts with Liberty. If she's alive, she's our matriarch."

Turning, he passed through the window and loped down the sidewalk. I didn't expect him to stop but he did. The look he gave me over his shoulder seemed like an invitation to follow.

Sinda offered to stay behind to deal with visits from contractors or the police, so Ren and I grabbed our things.

"This is so exciting," Ren said, as we hurried out to the car. "Until last month, I lived a monotonous life."

"You know what would make it even more interesting?" I asked, sliding behind the wheel and passing Bixby to her. “Coffee. We’ve got to find a way to heal Norm so that we can learn the intricacies of that espresso machine.”

“Isn’t that what Google is for?” Bixby asked, as he and Bijou jockeyed for position in Ren’s lap. “There’s a how-to on everything.”

“No way am I testing that machine unsupervised,” Ren said. “There are plenty of good reasons to forfeit your life in Wyldwood. Caffeine isn’t one of them.”

I laughed as I eased into traffic. “Speak for yourself. My withdrawal headache is bad enough to make me do something desperate.”

“We’d better fix that before the Christmas committee meeting,” Mr. Bixby said. “Or I don’t hold out much hope for jolly.”

CHAPTER TWENTY

Two hours later, I realized the joke was on us. The town wasn't large and we'd circled it a few times, looking for a ghost sheepdog who'd apparently decided to stay invisible.

"I failed the test," I said.

"Failed what test?" Ren asked. "We're driving around looking for an invisible dog. If that's a test, how can anyone pass it?"

Covering the last block to Whimsy at a crawl, I sighed. "Sinda thinks it's my fate to locate ghost dogs."

"Dogs that *want* to be found," Ren said. "Bixby was waiting for you and so was Bijou."

"Right right right," Bijou said. "Witchy was my ticket out and it took a billion years." She looked at me. "How much is a billion?"

"A lot," I said, finding a smile. "Sorry I kept you waiting."

"Short stuff was first in line," Bijou said. "He's your dog. I'm Renny-Ren-Ren's."

Ren gathered both dogs into a hug and my dachshund squirmed mightily in protest.

"I don't like the way that poodle feels," he said, as I pulled into my still-vacant parking spot right in front of the store. "So much useless fluff. It could smother a real dog." He gestured imperiously to me with one chunky paw. "My ride, please."

Picking him up, I smiled again. These dogs had brought such joy to my life and there was a chance Harold would, too. But not today, apparently.

"Harold deliberately duped me," I said. "That look was an invitation."

"An invitation to play hide and seek," Bixby said. "And you lost. It happens. So now we go back to plan A."

We got out of the car and walked back into Whimsy. Sinda was behind the counter wearing safety goggles as she worked on a new piece of jewelry. She had created a unique line of pendants for the store's opening and I had a feeling they were going to be a hit.

"No luck, I take it," she said, moving her tools out of the way.

"Duped," I repeated. "Every so often I got a glimpse of a tailless backside and then he was gone."

Sinda cleared the last of her things and then pulled off her goggles. "Perhaps Liberty isn't ready to be found. She's been missing a long time. It must be hard to trust."

"Especially with Shelley away," Bixby added.

"Good point," I said. "Harold is probably reporting in to Liberty and my recent performance wouldn't have inspired great confidence that I'd have her back."

"You're being too hard on yourself," Bixby said. "That's *my* job."

I set him on the counter and stroked his ears. "Thanks, buddy. I think."

Ren checked the window seat for Harold and then sat down carefully. "Bixby mentioned a Plan A. What is it?"

I went to collect *Everyday Spells for Everyday Magic*. "Ladies, welcome back to magic school."

Ren groaned. "I didn't like how things worked out the last time. Specifically, Mitzy is dead."

"Maybe she'll come back," Bixby said. "Janelle, did it ever occur to you that if you can bring over a dog, you could—"

"No. It didn't and I can't. If Mitzy's ghost shows up on the window seat, I guess we'll need to talk about it then."

Ren jumped to her feet and walked over to the counter, scowling. "Not funny, you two. That sounds very complicated."

"Unprecedented," Bixby said. "At least to my knowledge."

"And mine," Sinda said. "Think about all the cells you'd have to get just right. The margin for error would be very slim."

Setting the book down, I shuddered. "I doubt that's covered here. It's not everyday magic."

"You're not an everyday person," Bixby said. "Despite being a rank amateur."

Sinda shook her finger at the dachshund. "Good sir, there's a time for tough love and a time for encouragement."

Bijou left Ren and brushed up against my shins. "I'm here to cheer her on. Go, Witchy, go!"

I couldn't help smiling at her enthusiasm. "Thank you, Bijou, but we don't use that word, remember? And I'm not the only magical being here. Ren and Sinda have abilities, too. As do you and Bixby."

"Yeah, but you're the one with the book," Bijou said.

Now Ren smiled. "She's got a point."

"I keep wondering why this one got dumped on me." I ran my fingers over the pages and they flicked by quickly. Nothing jumped out at me that would bring back a long-lost cousin.

"Wing it," Bijou suggested. "Make something up."

"No!" Sinda's voice overlapped with Ren's.

Mr. Bixby just chuckled. "You've been told, Janelle. No improv."

"I'm sorry, dear friend." Sinda patted my arm and sent calming energy into me. "We've just seen how the slightest change can have unexpected consequences."

"I didn't blow up Mitzy," I said. "I'm sure of it. My stunning power only works when I'm super motivated. Like, life-or-death motivated. Plus I need direct contact."

"That was true before, but maybe things have evolved," Sinda said. "Are you the same woman I met in the park down south?"

I shook my head. "I don't even know that woman anymore. Till now, I've spent my whole life trying to repress this stuff." Touching the spell book again, I let the pages ripple under my fingertips until it finally settled on a spell. The illustration featured a cartoonish ox with exaggerated horns and a smirk. The title read, "Olly Olly Oxen Free."

"It is about hide and seek," Bixby said. "I told you."

I scanned the spell, barely mouthing the words. "*If you seek to hide from prying eyes, tap the emptiness inside and vanish with a simple ride.*"

"Uh, Janelle?" Mr. Bixby was craning to see out the front window. "I hate to be the bearer of bad news, but Elsa's gone."

"Gone! What do you mean, gone?" I stared at the empty parking spot. "My car's been towed?"

He tapped the book with his paw. "It's the spell, I imagine. You sent your 'simple ride' into hiding."

"Oh my gosh, I've vanished my car?" I ran to the window and looked both ways. "Elsa? Elsa!"

"Calm down and check the book," the dog said.

I ran back and tried to flip the pages but the ox stared stubbornly back at me. "I don't get it. This must be the right spell."

Mr. Bixby tapped again. "What does it say in the fine print?"

Under the ornately lettered spell was a tiny note in plain lettering: "Reverse as needed."

"Reverse as needed," I said aloud. "I need Elsa back. So, reverse please. Reverse!"

Sinda touched my arm once more, trying to calm me. "Take a little breather. I'm sure we can get Elsa back."

Bijou rose on her hind paws and danced around. "It's a trick. It's a trick. I like tricks!"

"Poodle, if you know the answer, say so," Bixby said. "Before Janelle melts down completely."

"Reverse as needed," Bijou said. "Read the words backward."

Ren shrugged. "Can't hurt to try, Janny. But you'll need to slow down and focus."

"Okay, okay." My breath came in short pants. "While I do this, can you guys be my eyes?"

Three voices murmured agreement and Bijou shouted "yes" three times, as usual.

"Just hurry," Bixby said. "In case someone takes your spot and Elsa lands on top. She'd crush a modern car."

I read the invisibility spell backward, sounding out each word in reverse. It was like reading another language.

Ren ran to the window. "It worked, Elsa's back."

"Oh, thank goodness." Sinda squeezed my arm harder. "And nothing was crushed."

"Hold the applause," Bixby said. "That old man has his phone out. Looks like he noticed your oopsie."

"Don't worry." Sinda's voice was reassuring. "Things like that must happen all the time around here."

Ren was still at the window taking inventory. "Uh-oh. Elsa's right front tire is missing. And her rear hub cap."

"What about the other side?" Bixby asked. "The driver's door, maybe? No wonder the guy's taking pictures."

There was urgency in Sinda's fingertips as she squeezed my arm harder still. "Repeat the spell, Janelle. I'm sure you'll catch the last bits of Elsa."

I nodded. "I probably mispronounced some of the words. Because they're not words."

"It sounded like Klingon," Bixby said. "Although I'm more Star Wars than Star Trek. As you know, or should know."

Sinda grabbed Bixby off the counter and walked away. "You're supposed to help, not hinder."

"I am helping." He struggled to get down. "I keep the mood light. She'd fall apart without my wit. I'm trying to show her everything will be fine."

"Everything *will* be fine," Sinda echoed. "Just read that line again, Janelle, and sound out every syllable slowly and carefully."

I did as she asked. It was like learning to read again. No doubt I had mixed things up the first time. Who wouldn't?

"The tire's back!" Ren applauded for real now. "And the hubcap, too. Well done, Janny."

"Better try that one more time and a little faster," Bixby said. "The car wasn't the only thing to appear with the spell."

I looked up from the book and he swept his long nose toward the window seat, where a collection of Australian shepherd parts sat waiting for assembly to be complete. There was an ear, one front paw, one rear paw and quite a bit of fur in between.

"Oh Harold, I'm sorry," I said. "Let me get your eyes for you."

Bixby laughed a little too hard. "Take your time. Serves him right for playing hide and seek."

My third reading in reverse flowed more easily. I was starting to see the collection of letters as words, and perhaps they'd soon have meaning, as well.

"We've got eyes on Harold," Ren said. "Once more for the missing ear and you're done."

The dog glared at me, probably disgruntled over being dragged out of hiding by a bungled spell. Unless I was much mistaken, he'd come reluctantly, fighting the whole way.

I shrugged at him. "Guess that'll teach you to take me on a wild goose chase. Keep it up and I'll give you a tail you don't want."

"Who wouldn't want a tail?" Bijou said. "Wagging is fun fun fun."

Harold turned his glare on Bijou and it was just as well he didn't speak.

Closing the spell book, I gave my friends a pleading look. "Could we not talk about this? At least for a while? I'm going to have post-traumatic spell disorder."

No one had time to answer before the phone rang. A glance at the screen told me my hope was futile.

CHAPTER TWENTY-ONE

"Hey, Mom."

"'Hey, Mom'? That's all you've got for me, Janelle Elaine Brighton?"

I didn't need to see her to know she was shaking her index finger. The middle name hadn't come out for a showing since Mom emerged from the bunker. I liked Gran's sister's name well enough but not when Mom weaponized it.

"How are you? And how is Gran?" I walked into the back room with the book and stowed it in the usual hiding place. Then I pressed a button on the phone. "I've got you on speaker, Mom. The gang's all here."

Having an audience might slow her caustic words, but probably not. Restraint didn't come naturally to our family. I'd worked hard for years to tame my sharp tongue, as had Jilly. We were the modern Brightons. Models of restraint.

"I am well aware that the gang's there, and that Elsa was not," Mom said. "I got a call from Midge Buckhorn saying she was about to pass your store when the bronze eyesore vanished from the street."

"Did Midge use the words 'bronze eyesore,' or are you dissing my car?"

"You know I never fall for diversions like that," Mom said, "although Midge and I happen to be in agreement about the car, if nothing else."

"So instead of checking in to see if we're okay, Midge decided to call you at the Briars and rat me out?"

"She could see you were okay. All of you milling about and tittering. She watched from a safe distance in case something else materialized on top of her."

I put the phone on the counter and slipped my arms into my coat sleeves. "Elsa is back and hopefully fully operational. I'll drive her to Tingle Square to make sure. The Christmas committee meeting convenes in fifteen minutes. And I'm on it. Ho ho ho."

Mom really didn't fall for diversions often, but this one she couldn't pass up. "Christmas committee? People are framing Ren for murder. You don't have time for such frivolities."

I held a finger to my lips to warn the others against letting Mom know the situation was shifting. "That's exactly what I told the mayor but she refused to take no for an answer."

There was a pause on Mom's end and Gran filled it. "Ruthann Longmuir wants you on the Christmas committee, Janny?"

"She does. The mayor made a point of speaking to me after she saw me in the municipal buildings trying to find information on Harold."

"Janelle." It was Mom again, and I sensed hands on hips now. "That's another thing you don't have time to worry about. You promised me you'd—"

"Behave?" I interrupted.

"Shelley, she has a point," Gran said. "Janelle's a grown woman and can make her own choices."

"She's a grown woman but not a grown witch," Mom said.

"Now, now. A late bloomer still flowers," Gran said. "It's better than too early. Look at my cousin."

Mom directed a huffing sound away from the phone, no doubt at Gran. "Can we not mention Janelle in the same breath with Cousin Liberty? The woman was deranged."

I scooped up Bixby in one arm and grabbed the phone. "Mom, people said the same of you when I got home. Did it occur to you that Liberty may have been poisoned as well?"

Pausing with my hand on the door, I let them chew on that for a moment. "Actually, it didn't occur to me," Gran said. "My cousin was always odd but more so before she disappeared. I wish I'd been more understanding." She sighed. "I suppose I can admit now that I was afraid of Liberty. My own cousin. She was erratic and superior and she scared me. There, I said it."

"Don't feel bad, Gran." I waved my phone at the others and walked through the door Ren held open for me. "Everyone's afraid of Mom, too. It runs in the family."

"Janelle Elaine Brighton," Mom said. "Your diversion game has improved considerably, I'll give you that."

I took her off speaker so that people in the street didn't have to hear the lecture. Small groups had clumped in various spots to discuss the vanishing car, and no doubt find out if the reassembled vehicle worked again. I sincerely hoped it would. Elsa deserved better from me.

"Mom," I said, unlocking the driver's door and depositing Bixby on the seat. "People are watching me get into Elsa and I'm feeling a little tense. Can we finish our chat after the committee meeting?"

My plea only made her pick up speed. "I told you not to play with that spell book. Nothing good can come of experimenting with magic unsupervised."

Sliding inside, I held my breath and turned the key in the ignition. The motor purred like a kitten and I patted the steering wheel gently. "Oh, Elsa, thank goodness. I'm so sorry about what happened." Pressing the speaker button on the phone, I set it on the seat beside Bixby. Then I pulled out into traffic, staring straight ahead to avoid the curious eyes of bystanders. "Mom, clearly I wasn't trying to make Elsa disappear. How do you target spells? It seems completely random."

Mr. Bixby had stayed uncharacteristically silent but he was done with that. "I suspect you're the random factor. It probably takes a great deal of focus. Am I right, Shelley?"

Mom didn't protest to Bixby using her first name, possibly because there were too many Miss Brightons. She had been married once, as had her sister, Eva, as well as Gran and Gran's sister, Elaine. All of them took their maiden name back after the relationships ended. Despite their complaints about the family, they were committed to being Brightons.

"The dog is right," she said. "It's crucial to be laser focused whenever you're so much as touching that spell book. Just a passing thought about the weather could bring on a storm. A negative feeling about someone could send them down a manhole. The book intuits what you want to do but it's like a driverless car. You need to keep your hands on the wheel, your mind on the road and stay within the lines."

That's exactly why I was still a little worried there was collateral damage from my growth spell around the time Mitzy died. My focus had seemed strong, but there was no way to be sure and fretting didn't help.

"Fretting never helps," Mr. Bixby said, on our inside line. "That's sort of the point."

"Okay, Mom. And speaking of which, I need to focus on the road right now. I'm a little nervous about seeing Oscar Knight at the meeting."

"Oscar? Mayor Longmuir threw you into his path? What is she thinking?"

Gran cleared her throat. The sound startled me because I'd

practically forgotten she was there. "Ruthann's a decent woman. A powerful woman. I would imagine she wants to keep a close eye on Janny. For her own good."

"For the town's good, you mean," Mom said.

"In the eyes of a politician, it's probably the same thing," Gran said.

I pulled into the municipal parking lot and backed into a spot close to the entrance.

"Planning for an easy getaway?" Bixby asked. "I like it."

Gran and Mom were still arguing at the other end when I said goodbye and clicked off quickly. The phone rang again immediately but I dropped it into my purse. Tucking the dog under my arm, I walked out of the parking lot.

Tingle Square, named after the town's founder, Orville Tingle, was always well maintained, but increasingly so as the holidays approached. There were plants in all the fall colors, some of which I'd never seen before. I wondered if they were artificial, but there were plenty of specialized greenhouses around. People depended on a wide variety of flora for more than aesthetics in Wyldwood Springs.

"This is one of those occasions where I'd love to stroll in on my own legs," Mr. Bixby said. "I'm more than just eye candy, you know."

"Far more. But I need you as close as possible to let me know when Oscar... Oh. Never mind."

I hadn't needed the dog to tell me a thing. The coiling snakes that always writhed in my mind, if not my very soul, when Oscar Knight was around made their presence known now.

"No need to connect with his jewelry anymore," Bixby said, sounding chipper. "Your abilities really are coming online."

"It's the nausea. Even though I can't see him yet, I feel him."

"Magical reflux. It's enough to make anyone queasy." He

shifted for a better look. "Chin up, swallow hard and smile. That's the mark of a true you-know-what."

In one corner of the square, three people had gathered. One was Becca Mathews from the pet store. The others were senior gentlemen I didn't recognize. All were wearing garish Christmas sweaters.

"I guess the mayor forgot that part," Bixby said. "You could have conjured something tacky out of hiding if you'd known."

"Stop it." I gave the dog a gentle squeeze. "I need to look confident. Remembering Elsa and Harold in pieces won't help."

Oscar and I approached from opposite directions. He picked up speed with his long, elegant stride to beat me to the group. His smile was subtly feral, as always, but he wore a jaunty blue scarf adorned with snowmen over his sports jacket.

"Janelle Brighton." His voice was smooth and pleasant. "Before I saw you I had this wave of— I don't know what."

"Nausea?" I suggested. "I felt the same way. It must be excitement over Christmas. We're going to have so much fun planning together, Oscar. I hope you don't mind if I use your first name, at least on the committee. We're all friends here."

His silvery eyebrows rose over gray eyes that verged on pewter. It was rare to catch him by surprise and I savored the moment.

"Don't savor too long," Mr. Bixby said, switching to our internal channel without my asking. Even the cheeky doxy had a healthy respect for Oscar. "Savoring leads to distraction, which we can ill afford this festive season."

"You're trying to join the committee?" Oscar said. "It's by executive appointment only. Mine, in fact, and I certainly wouldn't invite a Wyldwood newcomer to offer opinions on anything as important as Christmas. This is the biggest retail event of the year and your store isn't even open." His eyes narrowed. "May *never* open."

"Oscar, don't be a grinch." The voice came from behind him and he spun on expensive loafers to see Mayor Longmuir. She was wearing a muted green cardigan covered in Christmas trees that somehow made her more elfin still. "I invited Janelle to join us. We've all been doing this for years and it's time for an injection of fresh blood."

His smile somehow tipped down at one end and up at the other, possibly blending his disgust over my appointment and delight over her turn of phrase. For a moment, I wondered if the mayor had actually offered me to Oscar on a platter.

"We don't need a drop of blood spilled," Becca Mathews said. "Even if red is the signature color of the season."

The bald man beside her nodded. "This is about peace and goodwill. I'm happy to have the young lady and her handsome dog aboard."

Oscar's eyes left the mayor, canvased the circle of faces and landed on mine. "Fine. Welcome, Janelle. To the committee, specifically. I'm not sure what you can bring to it, being so new in town."

"New to Wyldwood—or at least new *again*—but hardly new to Christmas," I said, with what I hoped was a winning smile. "Mayor Longmuir probably knows I've organized massive Christmas celebrations at resorts all over the world. I have plenty of good ideas and a flair for PR."

He glanced at the mayor again. "I assumed there was a reason. So we'll give you the benefit of the doubt."

"Thank you, Oscar," the mayor said. Her smile didn't change but I felt something pass between them. It was evidence of their balance of power, I supposed. Without the mayor's tacit support, Oscar probably wouldn't be able to rule Main Street with an iron fist. Maybe he'd provided her with something important in return.

The other gentleman, who had a head of wild white frizz, signaled to the mayor and Oscar to join him, leaving Becca to close in on me with the bald man in tow.

"Janelle, I hope you plan to work hard," Becca said. "We lost

Candace Riordan and Ginny Steiner from the committee because of you."

"Because of me? Why would you say that, Becca?"

"The mayor dismissed them after what happened when you took over your store. Even though they were convicted of nothing. Candace and Ginny were Christmas mainstays. Worker bees. So Ruthann must think you'll pick up the slack for two."

Mr. Bixby gave my chin a little poke. I lifted it and threw my shoulders back for good measure before meeting Becca's eyes. "What happened at my store wasn't my fault, or I wouldn't be here on the mayor's invitation."

Straightening her garish pullover, Becca shrugged. "You have something Candace and Ginny didn't... a police chief in your skirt pocket."

"I'm sure Big Red would love to hear it phrased that way," Bixby said. "Although they are big pockets."

Ignoring him, I amped up my smile a little more. "Becca, I promise I'll work hard, even if I'm busy getting Whimsy launched. Joining the committee wasn't on my Christmas list, I must admit, but Mayor Longmuir wouldn't take no for an answer."

"Ruthann must want to keep an eye on you," Becca said. "Knowing you're a suspect in the murder of Mitzy Lennox."

"Leave it," Bixby cautioned me. "Leave it."

I tried to resist and failed. "I was nowhere near the Beanstalk Café when Mitzy passed, Becca. There must be a dozen witnesses to prove it."

"No one remembers that." She looked at the bald man for confirmation and he shrugged. His gaze was nearly as vacant as Norm Jenkins'.

Oscar Knight joined us in time to hear Becca's comment and I forced a little smile as I answered her. "People forget things sometimes. And then remember them later."

Tipping his head, Oscar smiled, too. "I wouldn't count on it this time, Janelle."

Becca leaned forward, until Mr. Bixby reached out and air-snapped to fend her off. "This situation had your name written all over it," she said. "Mitzy was frizzled, just like Reggie Corby when you attacked him decades ago. Same MO. Same reason."

"And what reason was that?" I asked. "In your opinion, I mean."

"Jimmy Barrow agrees," she said. "Then, as now, you were protecting your only friend, Renata Scott."

"You're wrong," I said. "Renata may have been my only friend in high school, but I have plenty of others now. Some you've seen, some you haven't."

Oscar looked curious but then he shook his head. "Becca, I understand you're upset about Mitzy, but now isn't the time. The mayor's asked us to focus on Christmas so let's keep things jolly."

"We need to help Ruthann see this is exactly what happened before, Oscar," Becca persisted. "Remember how Janelle went to defend Ren, and bang—Reggie was electrocuted. Now someone else goes after Ren, and bang—Mitzy was electrocuted. Can't be a coincidence."

He rested long fingertips on Becca's arm and she subsided. "Jolly, Becca. 'Tis the season."

I turned to Oscar. "I have wondered myself about the coincidence of people framing me. What do you think, Oscar? And how is Jared, by the way? Any chance he's back home for a visit?"

A maroon flush rose over Oscar's jaunty blue scarf. "I don't want to hear my son's name cross your lips, Janelle. Ever."

I shrugged. "Suits me fine, but I don't appreciate hearing speculation about Renata and me. You know a lot of people, Oscar. I bet you could get those rumors to subside."

"Possibly, but in my experience, it's best to let fires burn themselves out." He smirked a little. "The younger and hotter they flame, the quicker they die."

A chill ran through my limbs but I persevered. "Is that a threat, Oscar?"

Mayor Longmuir slipped into our circle. "A threat? Of course not, Janelle. Why so touchy? I invited you to join us so that you could have fun. And *be* fun."

I thought about letting it go, but the gleam in Oscar's eyes forced me on. "Becca and Oscar drained my fun bank by suggesting I had something to do with the passing of Mitzy Lennox."

"I suggested nothing of the sort," he said. "Not this time."

The mayor gave him a teasing smile. "Oscar, as I said, no grinches allowed. I know you have a big heart in there. You're a dog lover just like Janelle."

He rolled his eyes. "The ridgeback belongs to my wife."

The bald man beside Becca spoke for the first time, seeming to shake off a stupor. "Janelle, I knew your grandmother's cousin Liberty. Such a firecracker. You look just like her."

"I do? How interesting. I don't believe I've seen a photo."

"You Brightons are all lookers, if you don't mind an old man saying so."

I laughed and the mayor's elfin grin reappeared. "I don't mind, sir. I didn't catch your name."

"Gus Weeble," he said. "I run the hardware store."

"I met Liberty, too," Becca said. "She was quite pretty. I suppose that's how you Brightons get away with so much."

"More handsome than pretty in Liberty's case," Gus said. "She intimidated most of us. Maybe not Oscar."

I glanced up and found Oscar had moved a few yards away. He was bent over deadheading a flower display.

Gus continued anyway. "Bridie was always the friendly one. Bit of a beatnik."

"Gran is still a beatnik," I said, smiling.

"She's alive?" Gus asked, looking puzzled. "I thought they both died."

"Only Liberty," Becca said. "Bridie never really got over it. She wasn't eccentric before but she was afterward."

The mayor made a motion with her hand to interrupt. "People assume Liberty passed, but for all we know she's enjoying rum punch on a tropical island right now."

"You approved the estate sale, Mayor," Becca said.

Gus brightened. "I lived across the street then and got quite a haul of tools."

"I thought the Brightons were too good for a suburb like Kempville," Becca said.

"Nothing wrong with Kempville," I said. "I remember a pretty street with tall trees."

In truth, I remembered nothing. If I'd ever visited Liberty, it was before I was old enough to retain the details.

"Beechwood Boulevard," Becca said. "Liberty's house looked like a knockoff of the Brighton manor, complete with a gothic turret."

"I love a turret," I said. "Must be in our genes."

Mayor Longmuir stared at me and her eyes looked as green as her sweater. It seemed like she wanted me to know where Liberty Brighton had once lived. Perhaps there was something there I needed to find.

"Like a better spell book." Bixby had been quiet so long his voice startled me. "One for trainee drivers."

I couldn't help sighing. Unless I was much mistaken, I already had the beginner's manual.

Mayor Longmuir clapped to get Oscar's attention. "Huddle, people. Huddle! Time to debate the annual parade. To march or not to march?"

"Parades are a wee bit overdone," I suggested, gently.

"We *must* have a parade," Becca said. "It's tradition. Don't listen to Janelle."

"Respect, Becca," the mayor said. "We're here to make things merry in this town. That is my number one job."

"Good luck, lady," Bixby said. "Mission impossible."

Ruthann turned and sent a wink in Bixby's direction. It was blatant enough to make the dog and me give twin gasps.

"Oops," the dog said, hacking dramatically. "Did I just say that out loud?"

CHAPTER TWENTY-TWO

"The mayor's a witch?" Ren asked, from Elsa's back seat. She had gladly yielded the front to Sinda, partly out of respect, no doubt, but also because Bijou and Bixby didn't know how to share a lap amicably. Their squabbling would distract us from developing the solutions we needed.

"I hesitate to use a word like that over a wink," I said. "But it would explain how she keeps Oscar Knight in check. He did seem to have a respect for her I've seen for no one else."

"Maybe she knows what Jared did," Ren said. "And that's why she's taken you under her wing."

"Cape might be a better word," Bixby said. "You need a cape, Janelle. And a broomstick."

"Whatever the mayor's doing, I'm glad she's letting us look into this Liberty situation," I said. "I feel like I owe it to Gran. And Liberty's memory."

"Ruthann suggested Liberty might be sipping rum punch in the tropics," Bixby said. "A brazen hint she's alive."

"Or she wants Oscar to think so," I said. "Gran didn't talk much about Liberty but I got the impression she was one heck of a... you-know-what."

"Just own it." The voice came from the rear, but it didn't belong to Renata. When Bijou crossed over she was very sweet but she was finding her own voice and it was surprisingly frank. "The more you own it the stronger you'll be, Witchy."

I glanced over my shoulder. "Did you ever see Liberty, Bijou? You were on Main Street a long time."

The dog stared back at me with bright, round eyes. "She was nice to me."

"Nice to you! She saw you?"

"Don't know, but she always waved. Stopped and said hello when she had time."

Sinda turned and smiled into the back seat, too. "No wonder Liberty had a reputation, if she saw ghost dogs."

Bijou let out a heavy sigh. "I kept asking her to set me free but it didn't happen. 'Patience,' she said. 'Your day will come.' And finally it did."

"I guess the apple doesn't fall far from the family tree," Bixby said.

I shifted uneasily in the driver's seat and then urged Elsa on a little faster. Until then, Liberty had been little more than a name to me. Now I felt a tug of connection. Mom didn't see or care about ghost pets. In fact, like most of the family I'd heard about, she only saw Sir Nigel. Yet a cousin I'd barely heard about might have something rather notable in common with me.

"Liberty isn't drinking rum punch." Bijou's voice was nearly as small as when I first met her as a ghost.

"Is she dead, Bijou?" I asked, turning again.

The dog covered her face with her paws. "You tell me. I'm just a dog."

I reached a hand between the seats and touched her fluff. "Far from it, my friend. I guess we'll know soon enough. The mayor clearly wants us to check out the house and there may be clues."

Turning onto Beechwood Boulevard, I drove toward the turret

that stuck up among the trees. I'd expected the house to be in ruins, but it was in very good shape. It was also very much occupied. Three young children were jumping on a trampoline beside the house, screaming with glee.

"That throws a wrench into my plans," I said. "I thought we'd let ourselves in for a tour. Now we need to be invited."

"Time to work the Brighton charm," Ren said. "Sinda and I will throw what we've got behind you."

I parked in front of the house and turned off the engine. All three of us ran fingers through our hair at the same time and then we laughed nervously.

"Maybe you'll know them from the Beanstalk Café," I told Ren as we got out of the car.

"It's a bit of a hike from Kempville," she said. "But it's possible."

The dogs jockeyed for position ahead of us and were still bouncing off each other when we reached the porch. I found it more reassuring than irritating. They wouldn't be so goofy if we were in immediate danger.

Mr. Bixby turned his handsome brown eyes on me from the top of the stairs. "We're not the psychics, though. How do you feel?"

I ran my index finger along the iron railing as I climbed and then touched the brass door knocker. These metals didn't deliver a heavy load of impressions the way gemstones did but still, I couldn't deny the weight of the feeling that seeped into my heart. There was sadness here. Great sadness. My fingers clutched my throat and I fought the urge to cry.

"What's happening?" Ren asked, touching my arm.

"Someone died here. Maybe on this very porch." Fighting to catch my breath, I whispered, "My heart is breaking."

Bixby pressed a paw into my shoe to bring me back to the present. "Not today. We don't have time for historical heartbreak. Remember what we talked about earlier. Stay in your lane."

I nodded, but my hand dropped to my chest. "It hurts."

He pressed harder than a dog of his size technically could. "Do I need to come up and nip some sense into you?"

Sinda's touch on my other arm was refreshing, as always. It felt good to have two friends flanking me. "We could come back tomorrow, dear girl. When you've had time to adjust."

I stooped to collect Bixby. "Whatever happened here, I want to know. It has something to do with Liberty. My family."

Taking the brass knocker, I gave it a sharp rap. It brought a woman of about my age to the door. She had a baby on one hip, a toddler clinging to the other leg, and a tired look in her dark eyes.

"Hello there," I said. "I'm Janelle Brighton and these are my friends, Sinda and Renata. The dogs are—"

She cut me off before I was finished with the introductions. "I've heard your name. This house used to belong to a Brighton."

"I only learned that today," I said. "When I was meeting with Mayor Longmuir. Apparently my grandmother's cousin Liberty lived here for a time and I wanted to take a look around."

"Not today," she said. "It's naptime and the kids need a snack first. I have five under the age of eight. I don't have the luxury of giving tours to strangers."

She started to close the door and I shoved my shoe into the crack. It was becoming my signature move and one day my toes would pay a terrible price. "Please. I don't have a big family and it would mean a lot to me to see where my relative lived."

On the other side of the crack, her dark ponytail swished. "Bad things happened here. I can feel it every single day. If you come in it might get worse. Can you blame me for wanting to keep things safe and happy for my kids?"

I shook my head. It was hard for me to imagine having kids, period, let alone keeping five of them safe and happy. "Can't blame you at all."

The door eased off my foot and opened enough to show the baby's round brown eyes. "We felt so lucky to get this house for a deal. No one told us about the ghost. I thought real estate agents had to disclose things like that."

"Ghost? There's a ghost here?"

"There's *something* here. The wind blows through the house all the time, slamming doors and rattling windows even on a perfectly calm day. The kids don't seem to mind. In fact, they kind of like it, I think. But my husband and I don't get much sleep. Sometimes there's howling outside. Like a dog who's been abandoned. We love dogs and would get one except for the kids' allergies. Hearing that whining is—"

"Heartbreaking," I finished, already suspecting which restless dog lived here, making their days windy and their nights sleepless. "Maybe I could help."

She found a weary smile. "How exactly would you propose to do that? Are you a ghost whisperer?"

Bixby struggled to get down and I set him on his paws. Straightening, I gave her what I meant to be a reassuring smile. "If these disturbances have anything to do with my relative, maybe I could walk through the house and try to put her energy to rest."

She stared at me and then shook her head. "What if it got even worse? It's already so much worse this past month and I don't know how much more we can handle. If you'll excuse me, I really must go."

Pushing on the door, she squeezed my toes. Meanwhile, Mr. Bixby faded from sight and invited himself into the house to investigate for us.

"Would you let me hold the baby?" Ren said. "I love kids and your little girl is stunning. She could be in commercials."

The pressure on my toes eased. "People have said that before. But she's colicky and never sleeps. I blame it on the ghost but that never bothered the others."

Ren reached out and the woman relented, opening the door and letting her take the baby. "You need a night out," my friend said. "A nice dinner with your husband. What's your name?"

"Jules Skinner," she said. "Jeff and I haven't had a date night since Lara was born. We always wanted a big family but it isn't easy."

Ren gave Lara a moment to adjust and then introduced her to Bijou. The poodle went through her repertoire of tricks and eventually made both the baby and Jules laugh. I noticed little hoops with a sparkle of topaz in the child's ears and reached out to touch one.

The image of Harold racing through the house rose immediately in my mind. He was scaring the baby with his sheepdog busyness. I pushed back with comfort to let the little girl know he was just protecting the house. There was nothing to fear. She held her arms out to me and I took her from Ren.

"It's going to be okay, little one," I said. "All the wind will go away and you'll sleep so much better. You can relax, okay?"

Lara's eyelids got heavy almost instantly and I handed her back to her mother.

In the same moment, Mr. Bixby emerged from the house with his hackles high. There was a white ring around his eyes. I had never seen the dog look more alarmed.

"Huddle," he said. "Huddle! In the beater. Now."

"Jules, we'll leave you to tend to your crew," I said, wanting to escape before negative energy filled the baby again.

"Wait," she said as we turned to head down the stairs. "I'm sorry I was so short with you earlier. Please come in and take a look around."

"Nope," Bixby said. "And another two nopes for good measure."

"Thanks, Jules," I called as I followed my dog. "We'll take you up on that offer another time."

"Over my dead body," Bixby said. "Or Liberty's."

CHAPTER TWENTY-THREE

Mr. Bixby didn't get a chance to fill us in before Ren's phone rang. It was Ethan Bogart, and she let it go to voicemail so that she could hear what my dog saw in Liberty's former house.

Ethan called again, however, and then again. Finally, Bixby himself told Ren to answer. "But if this is about flirting I'll be very disappointed."

It wasn't about flirting. Ethan's voice was breathless but there wasn't a hint of romance when Ren put the phone on speaker. "Can you repeat that, Ethan? I can barely hear you."

"Someone's breaking into your store, Renata. I was dropping some stuff off in your dumpster, like you said I could, when I saw some dude going at your back door hard. He was making these weird sweeping gestures." He paused. "At least I think it's a dude. Hard to know in a hoodie, but I got him on video."

"Did he get in?" Ren asked. "Is someone in my store right now?"

"I don't think so. The guy pulled a screwdriver out of his pocket and started gouging at the door so I snuck into the alley to contact the police. Called Drew Gillock directly because I don't trust the rest of them anymore."

My foot got heavier and heavier on the gas and I mouthed some words of encouragement to Elsa. One minute the poor old girl was gone, the next in pieces, and now she was pushing it to the max for us.

"It's a car," Bixby said, from Sinda's lap. "Nothing more, nothing less. Unlike me, your traumatized canine hero."

Ren was still talking to Ethan when there was a sudden click. "I hope he's okay. He didn't even say goodbye."

"You can chastise him for his manners later," Bixby said. "After we figure out why someone chose your store to vandalize."

Sinda continued to smooth the dachshund's hackles but with each pass they'd rise again. "What do you make of those 'weird sweeping gestures'?" she asked. "Does that mean the vandal was trying to spell his way in?"

"Possibly." I was driving far too fast on Main Street. "Maybe the screwdriver is actually a wand. Do people really use those?"

"Something else to ask your mom," Ren said.

"Add it to my list. Either way, this vandal was getting frustrated when his efforts failed. Something I can relate to, unfortunately."

"Well, you've never taken a screwdriver to a door," Ren said. "You have the power to melt one, unlike this guy."

That perked me up considerably as we parked on a side street. There were two police cars out front and I wanted to bypass them if I could.

We ran through a lane and found Drew standing with his hand on Ethan's shoulder. The chef looked confused, but he brightened when he saw us. Hopefully that sentiment was about Renata.

Drew caught my eye. "How did you know to come?"

I looked from Ethan to Drew and back. "Ethan just called us. Said someone was breaking into Ren's place. Using a screwdriver, apparently."

"That's more than he told me," Drew said. "When I arrived he wanted to share his menu for the restaurant's opening night. Starting with escargot."

"Maybe mussels," Ethan murmured. "Then steak au poivre." Turning to Ren, he asked, "Mashed potatoes or scalloped?"

"Either would be good," she said. "Are you okay, Ethan? Did something happen with the screwdriver dude?"

His dark eyebrows came down. "Screwdriver dude? Is he one of your contractors?"

Ren turned to Drew. "What's wrong with him?"

Drew shrugged. "No visible head wounds but the paramedics are coming to check him out."

Bixby shifted under my arm and sniffed audibly. "They won't find anything unless they have a good nose for magical flatulence."

I moved a little closer and touched Ethan's wristwatch. "Thank you for calling us about the attempted break-in. We really appreciate it."

My words didn't trigger a memory of someone hacking at Ren's door. Instead, Ethan was picturing himself in chef's whites. The potatoes worried him greatly.

Bixby poked my wrist. "Do you smell steak? Spuds?"

I shook my head. As I traveled around with Ethan through his new bistro, I smelled only coffee. It was the same distinctive scent I picked up from Norm Jenkins and others. Ethan had likely been hit with the same memory fog, just moments after hanging up the phone on Ren.

Releasing his watch, I walked to the back door of Whimsy and signaled for Sinda to join me.

"Where do you two think you're going?" Drew called after me. "This is a potential crime scene."

I scanned my door. "No sign of damage here, Chief. You might want to check Ethan's phone. He said he got video of the vandal."

That distracted Drew long enough for me to use the key and we stepped inside. Then I locked the door behind me.

"Put me down," Bixby said. "When you're anxious you sling me around like I'm indestructible. Maybe I am, but there's no need to find out."

"The spell book, Bixby. We need to find something to clear Ethan's mind before they take him away. He may have seen Mitzy's killer. The spell I used on Norm wasn't enough."

The dog trotted over to the spot in the wall where I stored *Everyday Spells for Everyday Magic*. I touched the bricks and they slid open to reveal it.

"Always exciting to see that book," Sinda said, smiling. "Even when using it comes with such risk."

She was right. It was exciting to see and hold the book. There was so much energy percolating under its covers. Too bad my feelings of fear and inadequacy had to ruin the adventure.

"For now," Bixby said, using our inside line. "Not forever."

I couldn't take the book to the front counter as there would be at least a dozen bystanders by now, including some in uniform and possibly Officer Slick. Instead, I dropped to my knees and set the book on the floor. Opening it, I swept my hand over the pages and watched as they lifted, fluttered and settled on a pretty illustration.

It felt like I was staring into a clear blue pond from above. A silvery fish tipped slightly to look back at me and I could swear that its fins fanned gently.

"Janelle? Earth to Janelle!" Bixby's voice was commanding. "This isn't the time to fall into your own spell book with a big splash. No playing mermaid."

I touched my forehead with cool fingertips. "Whew. You're right. It was like the fish was calling me in and saying the water's fine."

He poked my arm. "Just memorize the words and put the book away."

Sinda touched my arm, too. "I daresay he's right, dear friend."

Luckily the spell was short and as clear as the water in the illustration. My own mind seem to declutter as I took the words on board. Then I started to slip the book into my bag.

"Bad idea," Bixby said. "We always get in trouble when you're running around with that thing."

"Bixby, I saw your eyes when you came out of Liberty's house. We're going to need the book. Aren't we?"

Instead of answering, he looked around the room. "At least grab a throw to conceal it. That book deserves more respect than it gets."

Sinda selected the finest of the bunch and helped me wrap the book up. There was barely room in my bag but I got everything settled and moved the bricks back in place.

Opening the door, I found Drew standing right outside with his hand raised to knock.

"All good," I told him. "No sign of intruders."

Drew directed his gaze at my eyebrows, as he often did, particularly when in close proximity. "I'll be the judge of that."

"And I'll be the judge of your romantic prospects, Red," Mr. Bixby said, sniffing around the chief's ankles. "They're not good if you can't meet her eyes."

"Don't you dare," I said, shaking my finger at the dog.

"Mr. Bixby," Sinda said, adding her disapproval to the mix. "That is so rude."

Drew looked down and backed away. "He'd lift his leg on me at a crime scene? What'd I ever do to offend him?"

"Let me count the ways," Bixby said.

I waved to send Drew inside. "Sorry. He's just being a jerk."

The dog strutted off. "I'm giving Big Red something to think about so you can get the job done with Ethan."

The chef was sitting on a stretcher reciting a recipe while being examined by two paramedics. Getting in there to try the spell was going to be tricky, and the way Ethan was rambling would get him fast-tracked to the ER for expensive and unnecessary tests.

"Can you create a diversion?" I asked my dog, as the area

behind the store became even more crowded with emergency personnel.

"Sure, I'll lift my leg on all of them," Bixby said. "Might take a while." After a moment, he chuckled. "Wait, I have a brilliant idea."

I never got to see what he'd concocted because a sudden wind picked up and started blowing trash out of the dumpster. Several broken bistro chairs rained down on the emergency staff, miraculously missing Ethan. Then a more localized cyclone forced the paramedics back and literally sent the stretcher rolling in my direction.

Stepping in front, I clutched my bag to my chest and let the stretcher crash into my midriff. No way would I put the spell book in the direct path of collision. Luckily, Sinda managed to dodge behind the dumpster.

"Whee," Ethan said, grinning. "This is fun."

I signaled Ren to try to hold back the paramedics and she shouted questions about Ethan's condition over the wind. Meanwhile, I took a deep breath, touched his shoulder and looked into his eyes. Somewhere inside, I could feel him watching me with the intensity of the fish in my spell book. It was an invitation to dive in and I didn't wait to be asked twice.

The spell was only two lines long and I managed to focus despite the hubbub Harold was creating all around me. That's what the sheepdog wanted, and I owed him my best shot.

Ethan caught the line I threw out, so I backed away mentally, reeling him in. When I felt his memories surfacing, I pulled my hand away and smiled. "How are you feeling, Ethan?"

He looked down at the stretcher and hopped off, brushing grit from his shirt. "What's going on? One minute I was watching someone break into Ren's place and the next... this. Did I get conked in the head?"

"Maybe," I said, as the female paramedic pushed past Ren and came over. I touched the woman's arm. "I bet she'll tell you there's no sign of injury."

"There's no sign of injury," the paramedic repeated, taking Ethan's pulse again. "But we should take you in anyway. You were talking gibberish. I never knew there were so many potato dishes. You have big decisions ahead."

"Potatoes Anna," Ren said. "That's my favorite."

Ethan flashed her a smile. "Done. Now, if you'll make me a coffee, Ren, I'll be as good as new."

"My espresso machine is too complicated," she said. "Haven't been able to get Norm Jenkins back here to do another run through."

Ethan straightened to his full six feet. "Why didn't you call me? Never met a coffee maker I couldn't master."

"Sir, we need to take you in to be checked," the other paramedic said, trying to catch Ethan as he walked away.

I snagged the guy's sleeve and said, "He's fine. You've done your job so well that Ethan's in perfect condition."

"Perfect condition," the guy repeated, and then slapped his colleague's shoulder. "We're good to go."

She nodded, picking up on his thought. "I guess we're done here."

"There are others in need," I said, releasing them to the wind. I could sense clarity coming to their minds and suspected they'd pass it on with everyone they touched. "If you have a moment, could you drop in on Norman Jenkins? He was even more confused than Ethan."

"Sure," she said, as the furry wind machine escorted them away. "We'll come to your opening, Chef Bogart. And if you hold those classes you mentioned, count me in."

"Classes?" Ethan wove through police officers to Ren's back door. "That's a good idea."

"You're probably committed now," Ren said. "I'll sign up, too."

Chief Dredger came out and confirmed no one had gained entry. We were safe to pass.

Ethan slipped behind the front counter and eyed the espresso machine. "Good model. Better than mine. Now I have a reason to stop by often."

Mr. Bixby made retching sounds. "Like we don't have better things to do than flirt."

"Quiet," Bijou said, prancing around joyously. "Let Renny-Ren-Ren have her moment."

Ren ignored both dogs. "Ethan, would you mind giving that machine a good once-over before trying it? Do you remember what happened to Mitzy Lennox?"

He gave her a strange look. "Of course, I remember what happened to Mitzy. I'm sure it was just a freak accident." He took the screwdriver Ren handed him and stared at it. "That guy trying to force his way in was using one of these. But it looked different. Old. With a wood handle." He slapped his pocket. "I caught it on video."

"There was no sign of it," Ren said. "Drew still has your phone."

I had seen the image of the vandal in Ethan's memory, but there was nothing to identify the person from behind. Whoever it was wore a black hoodie, jeans and gloves.

By the time Ethan had opened the machine, taken a look, and then shown Ren how to pull espresso, Drew had joined us.

"Smells good," he said.

Technically, I suppose it did. To me, fresh coffee was just about the finest smell on the planet, but not today. The slightly sickly smell from the memory spell had ruined it for me. I could only hope it was temporary as coffee normally brought me great joy.

Still, I took the little cup Ethan offered and fired back the scalding brew. If we were heading into trouble at the Skinners' house, I'd need caffeine to light a fire under me.

"Poor choice of words," Bixby said. "Although I wouldn't be

surprised if you needed to stun someone before the night's through."

When Ethan had served coffee to all takers, he rested his hands on the counter and smiled. "I feel like doing a test run of my menu tonight. Who's in?"

Renata's dark eyes told me it cost her something to decline. "Ethan, we're not free tonight, but I know of a family of seven who could desperately use a nice break. Would you consider cooking dinner for them?"

"Sure," he said. "I don't have a kids' menu, but I can fake something up. Tell them to come by around seven."

Her white teeth flashed. "That's awesome, I'll let them know. We'll take a rain check and happily sample potatoes in every shape or form."

Drew walked us out the back. "Care to share your plans? Because it's not safe for you ladies to be wandering anywhere."

"No wandering," I said. "We're heading back to the manor now. Everyone's beat. Hence the coffee."

"So beat," Ren added. "It's been a stressful couple of days."

Drew finally turned to Sinda. "You'll tell me the truth, won't you, old friend?"

"Who are you calling old?" Sinda gave him a playful shove. "Although today I'm feeling it, I confess. Can't wait to get into something more comfortable."

As she spoke, Bixby got into position to cock his leg on Drew's boot but a rather boisterous wind intervened and blew us on our way.

When I looked back, Drew was plastered against the brick wall, auburn hair disheveled. But there was no sign of confusion in his eyes now.

"Good one, Harold," Bixby called. "Every dog has his day. Get ready for yours."

CHAPTER TWENTY-FOUR

"She's alive, though, right?" I asked Mr. Bixby, as we all left the manor an hour or so later. I had gathered everything I thought we might need based on the sketchy details he'd provided.

The dog gave a delicate shudder under my arm. "I don't know that I'd go that far. She's there in some form or another, but she wasn't giving off vital signs. No smell. No sound. And a little further from 'human' than I've experienced."

"How do you even know it was Liberty?" I asked, as we got into the car. I passed the dog to Sinda, who was all in black, from head to toe. She looked at least a decade younger than when we met and was more agile, too.

Bixby's teeth chattered for a second before answering. "Let's just say you Brightons have a distinctive look, even in very difficult conditions. I'd speculate that she's dying a slow death from dark magic. There wasn't much left of her, but even as I watched, a hint of a spark lit up in her eyes. She knew who I was and knew you were nearby. But when she reached out with those ghastly... Well, you'll pardon me but I ran."

I rubbed his ears and felt the trembling. "You did the right thing, Mr. Bixby. I bet it will take more magic than I have to fix the problem. Later, once we've assessed the situation, we'll call Mom and let her run lead on the mission."

"Highly recommended." He sighed as he settled into Sinda's lap. "It's no wonder Harold has turned into a windmill. I was all aflutter and I don't even know Liberty. My obligation is to you but I have a duty to your family and friends as well."

Driving back to the Skinner house, I nodded. "You've already acquitted yourself admirably. So please stay safe tonight. And you too, Bijou. Harold is beyond agitated and you've seen the damage he can do."

The family was still there when we arrived, so we drove around the block and then parked in the bushes where we could watch. It was probably our one chance to get in and check things out. This family didn't stray far from home.

A half hour crawled past and then Jules came out with the baby. Lara was asleep and I flattered myself she was more at peace since our meeting of minds. The rest of the kids filed out from oldest to youngest, all clean, with slicked-back hair. Their dad came last and locked the door behind him. From a distance, he looked as worn and jaded as his wife. Living with a ghost and a trapped witch had taken a toll. Most would have fled long before now.

We waited another 15 minutes before we got out of the car and pushed our way through the bushes to the back of the house. A basement window was ajar but we stepped onto the porch first.

I'd expected more trouble getting in, but the door opened as soon as I touched the knob. It wasn't *my* magic that did it, however. There was a different vibration.

Perhaps Liberty wasn't as near death as Bixby thought.

"Oh, she is," he said, from around my ankles. "Liberty's on borrowed power. Yours, to be precise. I can feel her hovering on the fringes of your consciousness. Can't you?"

The truth was, I couldn't until he mentioned it. I had been tired since we visited earlier and now I knew why. Someone was tapping my magical mojo uninvited.

"Rude," I said, leading the others through the renovated kitchen and into the living room. Sinda and Ren were holding hands and I didn't blame them. My heart was pounding, too, but I had to put on a brave front for all of us. "Ask before taking, Cousin Liberty. I don't believe family trumps all. Just so you know."

There was no answer and I didn't anticipate one. I felt a presence in the room that was far more potent than Harold's and wasted no time pulling out my spell book. The ox illustration had gone from a smirk to a sneer, but I blocked it out and focused on reading the hide and seek spell backward.

I enunciated every syllable perfectly. Or so I thought.

Harold came into sharp focus sitting beside one of the battered old wingchairs that flanked the fireplace. The chair's occupant was far less defined.

What appeared was enough to make Sinda and Ren gasp behind me, however. It was less about what you could see than what you couldn't.

If this was the long-lost Liberty Brighton, there was very little left of her.

Still, Bixby hadn't been wrong about the family resemblance. The more I stared, the more I could see the lines of a face that looked very like Gran's. Her hair had likely once been very dark, also like Mom's and my own. As for her eyes, they were misty voids right now, but would no doubt be green. All the women in our family had green eyes—magical or not.

The misty eye sockets made Bixby shudder and I couldn't help following suit. Liberty wasn't fully human, but she also wasn't like any of the ghosts I'd met. And unlike Bixby earlier, I thought I could detect vital signs.

"Stolen from you," he said. "Not there before."

"Silence, dog." The voice was faint but commanding.

Bixby stepped forward, tail straight, ears perked and hackles up. "I will not be silent. My job is to protect Janelle and you're attacking her."

"I am not," the wingchair's occupant said. "She's my family. Why would I attack her?"

"To steal her spark. Her life force. Janelle's gone down by at least twelve percent today, in my estimation," he said. "She needs all of it so back off."

"Argue with a dog I will not," she said, shifting in the chair.

Sinda stepped forward, still holding Ren's hand. "Then argue with me. Know that I'll say the same thing."

"I won't argue with you, either. Whoever you are, you'd best stand back," Liberty said. "Janelle will recharge in due course."

"You don't know that," Bixby persisted. "You don't even know what you are."

There was a long pause, during which I eased Sinda and Ren out of the way. "I know what I'm not. And I know Janelle can help."

My fierce protector leaned out of my arms. "Then *ask* if she will. It's her choice to make." She started to speak again and he barked sharply. "Tell me Harold wouldn't do the same to protect you."

Liberty slumped backward as she took the hit. "He would. My sweet boy."

Harold rested his chin on what was likely her knee. A loose dark gown whipped around her skeletal frame. I had never seen anyone so thin before.

"You sent your sweet boy to get me," I said, feeling my energy stabilize. She had stepped away from the well, at least for the moment. "But he wouldn't explain why, although I know he could."

The Australian shepherd looked at me and spoke at last. "Not my place."

"I let him make his own decision," Liberty said. "All I asked was that he find out if the rumor about you was true."

"Which one? There are a lot of rumors about me."

"About rescuing ghost dogs. When I saw that dachshund, I knew." There was a long pause before she added, "I want you to do that for Harold. Please."

Ah. So that was it. We truly had something in common.

Harold and I exchanged a long look and came to an understanding. "He doesn't want to be free, Cousin Liberty. If I call, he won't come."

"He will. Harold, I demand you go with Janelle. Live the life I promised you before he took it."

Harold turned resolutely away and collapsed at her feet, such as they were.

"Who took Harold's life?" I asked. "And yours?"

Her hand lifted in a weak gesture of dismissal. She was already paler, probably just from stopping the pull on my energy. "Oh, who else? Oscar Knight. His grandfather and father had a grudge against our family and so it goes. It's the way of our world."

She nearly vanished and I stepped forward. "Take five percent of my energy and finish this story, Cousin Liberty. It's important for me to know."

"Five percent is too much," Bixby said. "Harold wouldn't give you five of hers. If she had any to give."

There was a hollow sound that approximated laughter from the wingchair. "He's right, this snotty little familiar of yours. Harold wouldn't give you an iota of my energy. But I'll take what you're offering freely because it might help you keep your mother alive."

"What about Gran? Your cousin."

She sniffed. "Oh, Bridie. We were close once, but eventually she got as snotty as your dog. Like it was my fault I was always getting hit with the Knights' petty spells. People thought I was eccentric, when I was sick."

"Aha! That's what I figured. Mom was very sick recently and

Oscar was behind it. So yes, it would help if you could tell me what happened."

Tapping far more than five percent of my energy, she rose out of the chair and paced with Harold at her side. "Oscar came with half a dozen acolytes and cast a terrible wasting spell on me. My sweet boy took part of the hit, so it didn't quite kill me, although Oscar believes it did." She stopped pacing to stare at me and for a moment I saw the Brighton green of her eyes. "He left Harold to die."

I gasped. "That's terrible."

"This dog wouldn't leave me. He guarded the house for days, even weeks, until finally he passed on the porch. After that, he could come in, of course, and we've been together ever since. Decades, I would imagine. I have so little sense of time, but you were just a baby when it happened. Your mother came but she couldn't see us. She's not half the witch you are, despite all your dithering."

"See?" Bixby said, glancing at me. "I keep saying you sell yourself short."

"Untrained, undisciplined, unwilling," Liberty said. "All the 'uns' that will lead you to this: unhuman."

"You sent Harold to get me," I said, ignoring the taunt. "How?"

"He's a sheepdog," Liberty said. "Being bound to this house would have driven him insane. So I used the last bit of my magic to let him move around. It was the least I could do for the best dog in the world. But now I want you to bring him back. Give him the life Oscar took."

I shook my head. "It only works if they want to cross. So to get Harold to come over, you need to come, too."

"Impossible," she said, collapsing on the wing chair. "He needs to come over and help protect you. The living Brightons. I insist." She turned to the dog. "Harold, I have nothing left."

Walking over with Ren and Sinda on either side, I faced her.

"You have me. You have Mom and Gran. You have my friends and our dogs. And the second-best dog in the world."

"Third," Renata said. Her voice had a quaver, but she was assured nonetheless.

"Another un-witch," Liberty said. "The other one's a little better."

"Thank you," Sinda said. "Harold is on my list to bring over, Miss Brighton. He is slated to come back via Janelle, so I suggest you pack up for transfer."

Liberty's hollow eyes parked on Sinda and my friend didn't flinch. "Impossible," the elder Brighton repeated. There's not a spell in that book that would do it. I know, because I wrote them."

I clutched the book to my chest. "Everyday Spells for Everyday Magic? It's yours?"

"It was my beginner's manual, which I left with your Gran for you. She didn't know she had it, so she didn't know when it was stolen. But it ended up where it belonged, as I figured it would."

"How do you know all this if you don't leave the house?"

"Harold," she said, sinking into her chair again. "He gets around and brings back the information I need. True to breed, he likes to stay busy."

Mr. Bixby issued an order on our inside line and I pulled the other wingchair around to face my relative. "We don't have long, Cousin Liberty. Let's get you on the next shuttle to the land of the living."

Her wispy hair swished. "Your novice is showing. It would take every ounce of energy you have and then some."

"I bet we can figure something out," I said, as my friends murmured encouragement. The pages of the spell book fluttered under my fingertips. "Ah. The growth spell. Can I grow my powers enough to bring you over?"

Her sigh blew clear across the living room and lifted my hair.

"What a waste of your good energy," Bixby said. "I don't like this one bit."

"I don't either," Liberty said. "I appreciate the gesture, Janelle, but I'd be a poor excuse for a family matriarch if I let you sacrifice your life for mine." She looked down. "Harold won't hear of it, either."

I tried flipping the pages of the book but it stayed stubbornly open at the growth spell. "Your book—now my book—has spoken. We're going to grow my powers, bring you and Harold over and then join forces with Mom to beat down Oscar Knight once and for all."

This time her laugh sounded noticeably stronger. "I do like your spirit, but I also heard what you did to my dog. He was missing an ear for some time."

"That's where you come in," I said. "I have a duty to rescue this dog. How about you stop being unwilling, unavailable and uncooperative—all the 'uns'—and help me do what I'm here for?"

I felt a little tug in my chest as she pushed herself to her feet. She was tapping well over 12 percent now and it was bound to get worse.

"I'm not sure I like you," she said. "Young witches had more respect in my day."

"I'm not a witch. I hate that word."

"Oh yes you are, young lady. Despite your silly lexicon, I'm sorry to say you're very much a witch." Her fingers were discernible now as she pointed. "And that is very much a wiener dog."

"When you're alive again I'm going to bite you," Bixby said. "You old hag."

"Take it up with Harold, short and sassy," she said. "Now, are you going to be part of the problem or part of the solution?"

"Lady, your life is in my paws," Bixby said, demanding to be in my lap. "Because I'm the one driving this show."

CHAPTER TWENTY-FIVE

Bixby wasn't far wrong, as it turned out.

The spell worked—perhaps a little too well. I pictured the exact result I wanted, seeing myself grow in power and brilliance and feeling the change.

The only problem was that as fast as I could grow it, Liberty took it. At first I thought it was intentional. That she was stealing more than she needed because she could. But then I intuitively felt that she was just desperately thirsty. Her off switch had broken and she was gulping like someone drinking from a firehose. Maybe she didn't know the well had a bottom but she was getting very close to it when I said, "Stop."

Only the word didn't come out. It had gone past that already. I couldn't speak aloud and sunk deeper into the wingchair. I was fading out of life, just as Liberty had.

But I had something she didn't.

Friends.

Community.

Bixby.

"Stop, stop, stop," Bixby said. "You're draining her, lady. Back off!"

I watched as if from far away, as Ren and Sinda shook Liberty, who now looked fully human again, although her eyes were closed. Her fingers, once nearly invisible, clutched the arms of the chair and she nearly convulsed.

Neither of my friends had any effect on Liberty and I got weaker and weaker, until Mr. Bixby climbed onto the arm of my chair, stared at me and said, "Burn her. Shock her. Zap that energy-sucker, now."

"Can't," I told him silently. "Don't know how."

"Janelle Brighton, I did not cross back over to watch you shrivel up and blow away because your so-called matriarch can't control her appetite. Boundaries! Give her a slap she'll remember. Do it for Ren and Sinda and maybe even Drew. But especially do it for me."

He took my wrist in his mouth and gave it a shake, like one of the creatures he was bred to kill. The prick of his eyeteeth was just enough to get me back on my feet, metaphorically speaking.

Searching around inside myself, I found a spark. Just an ember that turned into a tiny flame, flickering in the darkness and the wind.

"There," Bixby said. "Grow it."

That's what I did. I repeated the growth spell once more and watched the flame expand until it warmed me fully, from heart to fingertips.

And then I pushed.

Hard.

So hard that Liberty's wingchair tipped over backward and her lace-up Oxfords stuck up in the air. There was a scramble of limbs and her hair, so similar to Gran's long locks, appeared over the seat. She jumped to her feet as easily as if she were my age. I had become hers, it seemed, because I couldn't move.

"What just happened?" she asked.

Bixby jumped out of my lap, stalked over and bit her shin. "You just about killed your cousin, you greedy old hag. That's what happened. I knew you couldn't stop yourself."

Harold started to whirl into a furious cyclone and I found my voice. "Harold, no. That's what Bixby is here to do. And what you are here to do for Liberty."

Cousin Liberty hopped around and rubbed her leg and then looked down. When she saw Harold, she let out a heartrending howl that he echoed.

"Stop that noise, both of you," Bixby said. "Do you want the neighbors to call the police? How will you explain all of this?"

"Harold," Liberty wailed. "He didn't cross, Janelle. Do something!"

"How can she do a thing with what you left her?" Bixby snarled. "She can't even get off the chair. It's your fault, Liberty. You have nothing and no one to blame but yourself."

"Bixby, don't," I said. I could feel the agony coming off the old woman in waves. "She didn't know. She didn't do it on purpose."

"I want to go back," she said. "Take it all back and I'll go."

I shook my head. "It's a one-way trip. But I can bring Harold over if you'll just let me get my strength back."

"The tea," Bijou said. "Give her the tea, Renny-Ren-Ren."

Ren dropped to her knees and fumbled in her backpack. She pulled out a thermos and held the mouth of it directly to my lips. "Drink up, my friend. Your mom puts some sparkle in it."

"Levenclaw," Liberty said. "I smell it."

I felt it, whatever it was, and gradually, I perked up.

In time, I have no doubt I would have fully recovered and fulfilled my destiny of bringing Harold together with Liberty on this side of the divide.

Unfortunately, among all the hubbub and howling, we'd acquired company. When the scent of levenclaw faded, I smelled coffee.

More specifically, I smelled hickory, with notes of caramel and molasses.

"Renata, move," I yelled, although it came out as little more than a whisper. It was enough. She bolted out of the way just before someone all in black jabbed at her savagely with a screwdriver.

Bijou leapt at the attacker and as he tried to aim a kick at her, Harold blew into a twister and pushed him back.

The ghost dog wasn't enough this time. The man with the screwdriver had magic on his side, and likely some mania as well.

"Recovery time's over," Bixby said. "Get your butt moving, Janelle."

I pushed myself out of the chair, pulled it around in front of me and stowed the spell book underneath. Gesturing for Ren, Sinda and Liberty to move into a line behind me, I called out, "It's six against one, Diggory Waring. You lose."

The man laughed. "Six? You need another puff of the good stuff, lady. I see three feeble witch wannabes and an old lady who was dead and will be again. Mr. Knight is on his way."

"Good," Liberty said. "I look forward to seeing him again. And I look forward to being the last thing he sees. Because if either of you come near Janelle, well, I'm afraid a wasting spell will be your dream come true."

"I can't kill the old lady again till he gets here," Diggs Waring said. "I promised to hold dessert for him if the mayor's hint was true. But he said I could take out the rest of you."

"Why?" I said, stalling less for time than for my strength to return in full. "What does Oscar have against me?"

"That's between him and you. But he wants his building back, which you apparently tricked out of him. The mayor won't let him take drastic action, so I offered to do it for him."

I crossed my arms. "Now, wait. Didn't Mitzy Lennox make that same offer? And what happened to her?"

His face turned pale and then flushed red with such ferocity it must have felt like I did a few moments ago when flame filled me.

"Don't compare Mitzy Lennox with me," he said. "She got in over her head. Owed Mr. Knight back rent and got further behind because of losing her staff." He jabbed the screwdriver in Ren's direction. "Starting with that rat leaving a sinking ship and siding with the enemy." The screwdriver jabbed my way. "But Mitzy had no game. Not a bit of magic to help, poor thing."

"And then she had the audacity to try to limit your business," I said. "Telling you who you could supply with beans, when her café was failing. I'm sure you had to bring her up sharply."

"She had it coming," he said. "Should have just stabbed her, like I'll stab you. Magic is messy—always so many implications you don't expect."

"Don't I know it," I said, laughing. "Maybe you heard about what I did to my car."

He laughed, too, although it was far from a pleasant sound. "It told me what I was up against. Pretty much nothing."

"I'm afraid so. I do my best, but it normally backfires. I don't imagine you expected so much drama from the exploding espresso machine."

"It worked better in theory. Mr. Knight arrived right after, and boy was he mad. Take it from me, you don't want to see that. I had to come up with a fix super fast. But I did and it's working so far."

"The memory spell," I said. "Took me a bit to figure it out. I'll never feel the same way about coffee again. At one point it was my greatest love."

Diggs Waring stared at me. "It's a good thing I planned to kill you anyway. And just so you know, Mr. Knight added a little oomph to that spell to make sure it did what it should."

"That is good to know," I said. "Regardless, I've already started reversing the memory spell. Did you know it works like a virus?

Eventually it'll hit everyone you did and I guess it'll be interesting to see how Oscar feels about things then."

"I doubt he'll be happy," Liberty said, speaking for the first time. "Just based on what he did to me for far less."

"It took Oscar and six other people to put you out of commission, right Cousin Liberty? I'm guessing you were a strong lady in your day."

"Some said so, yes. But they have no idea how strong I am today. I've had decades of rage and a nice infusion of something else to fuel me. Can't wait to tell Oscar all about it."

Diggory Waring had lost his swagger, but it was replaced by something worse: desperation. He realized he was going to need to remove both Liberty and me from the equation before Oscar arrived.

"Yeah, good luck to you, Beans," Bixby said. "Have you got your mojo back, Janelle?"

I wasn't sure. The tea had helped, no question. Time had helped. And the same thing that motivated Diggs Waring was also motivating me: desperation. I would protect those I loved with my life, no questions asked. But before I made any bold moves, I had an obligation to fulfill.

Turning to look for Harold, I let my guard down for Diggs Waring. Taking the opening, he lunged for me with his screwdriver. He nearly landed the shot, because it still felt like I was moving through deep water. I managed to dodge a few inches before shouting, "Harold, come!"

I pulled, hoping I had what it took to haul the sheepdog back from beyond. If I succeeded, this dog would be a powerful force working on behalf of my friends and family. He was formidable as a ghost and would be even more so alive again.

For a long moment, it felt like I was losing the battle. My strength ebbed. But then three sets of hands landed on my shoulders, and we all pulled together.

The whirling, twirling cyclone of wind climbed onto the chair barrier and then leapt. Diggs Waring stabbed wildly but the screwdriver hit air, and by the time it became real tricolor hair, the man was down.

Two Brighton women stood over him, with a sheepdog and a dachshund. The fear in his eyes was replaced with fury and he took a wild swing at Bixby. The dog dodged it easily, but the fury was contagious.

"Mistake, Diggs," I said, bending and jabbing with a forefinger. "Big mistake."

Bending was also a mistake, as it happened. I delivered a pulsating shock strong enough to disable Diggs Waring, but then I tipped and fell forward.

When my palms landed on his chest, I felt the reverberation of my own stunning shock and for a second, everything went black.

CHAPTER TWENTY-SIX

"Give her another shot of tea," Liberty said, as the face above me became clear. It belonged to Mr. Bixby, and his brow was furrowed in concern. When I blinked and swallowed, however, his expression changed instantly to typical nonchalance.

"No more tea, thanks," I said. "I already need to use the loo and that would be weird in someone else's house."

"It's my house," Liberty said. "Belonged to another Brighton cousin, once upon a time."

I sat up. "But the house sold to the Skinner family after you were legally declared dead."

"Well, I'm very much alive and buying it back will be my first priority." She was kneeling beside the writhing sheepdog, mumbling endearments. "Harold had plenty of time to find out where the bodies in this town were buried. And the bullion. I don't anticipate a money crisis any time soon."

"We have other crises to deal with at the moment," Renata said. "Is Diggory Waring dead?"

"Unfortunately not," Liberty said. "Do you always pull your punches, Janelle?"

I nodded as I pushed myself to my feet. "I have no desire to kill anyone. If the past is any indication, he'll be too befuddled to cause more trouble."

"And too befuddled to regret what he did," Liberty said. "Which is the whole point, is it not?"

"I don't make the big decisions," I said. "Just disable immediate threats."

She didn't move out of the way as Ren and Sinda tried to push the chairs upright. "I hope you'll make big decisions when Oscar gets here. Or have the good sense to leave them to me."

I tried to catch her arm but she jerked it out of reach. "Cousin Liberty, we can't take on Oscar Knight right now. You're just back and I'm rather depleted."

"Because of you, old lady," Bixby said.

Harold growled at my dachshund and Bixby growled back. Bijou came up beside my dog and added her growl to the din. Turned out the original rescues were closer than they let on. Hopefully Harold would join our ranks. If he brought his gift of wind over, he'd be a huge asset.

Finally, Liberty met my eyes. "Like it or not, I'm the senior Brighton here and I'll make the decisions about what we do in the face of an enemy. Especially one who trapped me for over thirty years."

"We don't like it," Bixby said. "Being the family elder means you should have more wisdom."

"Bixby, it's okay," I said. "She's still recovering from a terrible ordeal. And while that's the case, I'm making the decisions, Cousin Liberty. After all, you wouldn't be here right now without me, right?"

Her lower lip jutted but the one she cared about most took over. "She's right, Miss Brighton," Harold said, his voice both strong and quiet. "Patience was never our strong suit and it got us in trouble, didn't it?"

That turned Liberty's pout into a grin. "It sure did, old friend. I daresay impatience is what landed me on house arrest. I didn't have powerful friends and the only family member with magic was Shelley. She had her hands full with Janelle. And Janelle's deadbeat dad."

I pressed my lips together. Now was not the time to chase red herrings. Besides, there was a note of pain in Liberty's voice that told me she'd felt very much alone in the world. That was probably what made her want to take on too much too soon.

"You have plenty of friends now," I said, gesturing to Sinda, Ren and the dogs. "And before you say anything snippy about us, just remember we've put Oscar in his place before. Even the mayor noticed."

"It's a moot point," Bixby said. "Oscar is a no-show. I'd smell magical flatulence. Once Beans here passed out, the bad gas dispersed."

"Magical what?" Liberty said.

"He's right," Harold said. "Little guy has a good sniffer. I got a whiff of sulphur and decomp."

Bixby inclined his head modestly. He was willing to overlook the "little" in favor of the compliment from an impressive dog.

I scanned my mental space and confirmed the dogs' impression. "Oscar must have changed his mind. I'm not sensing the snakes."

Liberty perched on one of the chairs, now sitting where we'd found it. "Shame. I was hoping to polish him off today, while I still have a head of steam."

"He probably heard the police sirens," Ren said. "I texted them when Diggs arrived."

"The regular police?" Liberty crossed her arms and smiled. "This ought to be interesting. How about I just sit here quietly and let you explain everything? Harold told me you're sweet on the visiting police chief."

I sighed. "This is going to be complicated and I really would appreciate it if you sat quietly. Drew and I are just friends but I don't like lying to him."

"There's no need to lie when you can just wipe his mind clear," Liberty said. "That's how we've been managing such incidents for generations. No need to reinvent the wheel, Janelle."

"No wiping," I said. "It's disrespectful. Let me handle it."

She threw herself back in the chair. "Fine. But do handle it."

I scooped up Bixby just before more than a dozen boots clomped into the room. Ren and Sinda came up on either side of me and looped their arms through mine. Harold left Liberty's side to circle and draw us closer together—a simple move that told me he was grateful, and that we were indeed a team.

Drew Gillock stared down at Diggory Waring, who was awake now and mumbling inanities at the ceiling. The word "beans" came up over and over. That was probably the extent of his world now that I'd adjusted his mental circuitry.

The chief's dark eyes scanned the room, eyebrows rising as he encountered Liberty's little smile, and then turned to me. "Care to explain what happened here, Miss Brighton?"

"I do want to explain, Chief," I said. "It's a bit of a strange tale."

Drew sighed. "Aren't they always? The cases where you're involved are very strange indeed."

I sighed, too. "I do find myself in the wrong place more frequently than I'd like, Chief. Tonight, we came over to make sure the Skinner family left on time to enjoy their dinner at Ethan's new place. We decided spur of the moment to offer to babysit for them."

"That would have been so fun," Bixby said. "Not."

"Please tell me the kids aren't here," Drew said, eyes narrowing. He was willing to cut me a bit of slack but not if innocent children were involved.

"They were driving off as we arrived," I said. "But then we saw this dog—a stray we'd seen elsewhere a few times—walk right inside. I knew he didn't live here. Jules Skinner said the kids have allergies, and he has a lot of hair. So we decided we'd better do something about it."

"I see. So you just broke in to deal with the dog."

I managed a smile. "You know how I am with dogs, Chief. But Harold wouldn't come willingly. We got into a bit of a scuffle."

"Harold?" Drew said. "You've already named him."

"I named him," Liberty said. "He's actually not a stray but my dog. Harold would never leave me."

"And you are...?" Drew's coppery eyebrows came together, telling me he already knew, or at least suspected. There was probably a fat file on Liberty down at the police station.

"Liberty Brighton," she said. "Recently back from a long trip abroad." She swept her arm around. "Welcome to my home."

Drew reared back. "This isn't your home, ma'am. It's belonged to the Skinners for some years."

"Oh, I know. They were temporary caretakers while I was gone. Now, we'll find them somewhere more suitable for children." She glanced at me. "My young cousin will take care of my affairs."

I wasn't her personal assistant, but there would be time to establish our roles later.

"Let me recap, Janelle," Drew said. "You happened to drive by and saw the stray dog enter the house. You followed and found your long-vanished cousin reclining in a wingchair."

"I never recline, young man," Liberty said. "Posture is everything. Even at my age."

His eyes briefly took in her dress. Though dated, it had come through the ordeal in good shape. More importantly, it fit properly again. She had clearly fleshed out to her former glory.

"On your meal ticket," Bixby pointed out. "She'd better make it up to you."

Liberty's eyes—the youngest thing about her—landed on Bixby and squinted, but she settled for a pucker of disapproval.

"My cousin had arrived home from—"

"Abroad," Liberty supplied.

"Just moments before we got here," I said. "To say I was shocked doesn't begin to capture it. I've always thought she had—"

"Died," Liberty said. "I don't pussyfoot around the word death. It comes for all of us eventually. But apparently I still have some time to enjoy Wyldwood Springs."

"Interesting," Drew said. "I'm obliged to point out that you're all trespassing. And I assume you broke in."

"The basement window was ajar," I said. "We just followed the dog." Both things were technically true, although Liberty had borrowed my magic to unlock the door. That was much harder to explain to police.

His next sigh was more exasperated. "And if this family reunion weren't exciting enough... you ran into Diggory Waring. And he ended up babbling about coffee beans. Please do fill me in on that."

"Diggs killed Mitzy Lennox," Renata said, picking up the tale. "He confessed to rigging her espresso machine, and was probably planning to do the same to mine earlier today if Ethan hadn't intervened."

"He had an alibi," Drew said. "Oscar Knight vouched for him."

"Since when did Oscar's word count for anything?" Liberty said. "Perhaps he developed more integrity while I was abroad, but I doubt it."

"He killed Mitzy," I confirmed. "He told all of us so."

"Did he say why?" Drew asked.

Ren started to speak and I pinched her arm gently to let me continue. "He was outraged that Mitzy was trying to limit his business. The Beanstalk Café was in trouble and Mitzy owed back rent to Oscar Knight. So Diggs wanted to branch out and when she stopped him from supplying his organic beans to Ren, he lost it. I expect he owes money to Oscar, too. A lot of people do, we've heard. It creates tension."

"But that doesn't explain Mr. Waring's current state," Drew

said, as the paramedics pushed a stretcher into the room. "It sounds like you were just having a chat and then... this."

"He attacked us and we pushed back. Four against one, you see. I suppose he hit his head when he fell."

"And now he's mumbling nonsense. Just like all the others," Drew said.

"What others?" Liberty said. "I must have missed a few details."

I glared at her. "We have so much to catch up on, Cousin Liberty. Now is not the time."

"I'm sure your cousin would like to hear all about it," Drew said.

"Yes indeed, but not from you." Liberty stood up and came over to stare at him. "You're overreaching, Andrew. Overreaching in every way."

"Cousin Liberty! Please be respectful of Chief Gillock."

She flicked her fingers at Harold. "I've lost patience. This is boring and I didn't come back to be bored, Janelle." After the sheepdog got the police rounded up in the center of the room, she added, "You've had your chance, and now I'll deal with this."

CHAPTER TWENTY-SEVEN

Mr. Bixby sat on the marble island in the manor's kitchen, still chuckling. "Big Red looked as dumb and placid as an ox."

"Never mind," I said. "I'm not happy about what you did, Cousin Liberty. Not happy at all."

She shrugged as she strolled around wearing one of Mom's dresses and a pair of her shoes. They fit her well, but she looked uncomfortable.

"Of course, I'm uncomfortable," she said, reading either my mind or my expression. "Your mother always had terrible taste. Apparently, you inherited that from her."

I thought about arguing but wouldn't give her the satisfaction. All Liberty wanted to do was argue. She was the opposite of me.

"Maybe you should argue more," Mr. Bixby said. "You've been holding in a lot of opinions for a long time, too."

"No need to hold back opinions now," Liberty said. "I'm here on janitor duty, cleaning up what you won't, Janelle."

Renata looked young and small on her stool, clearly intimidated by my relative's feisty personality.

Sinda, on the other hand, got up and crossed her arms. "Liberty, we all understand what you've been through, but I can't allow you to disparage my friend."

"You're my age, Sinda. Janelle is too young to be our friend."

Sinda smiled. "I daresay I'm older than you, but Shelley's tea has worked wonders for my complexion. Regardless, I'm a close friend of Janelle's and you could be, too."

Liberty rolled her eyes. "I don't understand all this new age blather, although I watched enough TV with that passel of Skinner kids. Janelle is my blood and that's that."

I shook my head. "That's not how I operate, Liberty. I choose my friends very carefully and they become my family. Sharing a last name isn't enough to earn my loyalty—especially if you're going to disregard my explicit requests."

Her lips puckered and she would have continued to argue if Harold hadn't pressed against her legs and herded her toward me. "Fine, I'm sorry I slapped your boyfriend with a memory spell. He'll forget the details of what happened at the Skinner house, but I'm quite sure he'll remember you, if that's what you're worried about."

"Drew is my friend, and he's helped me in ways you can't. I owe him more respect than to meddle with his mind. There are always downstream implications with magic."

"Not always. I'm far more skilled than Diggory Waring with his inept coffee fog." She stopped in front of me and smirked. "I'm sure it will be fine, although you may lose attraction after seeing Andrew's bovine expression."

Bixby started to laugh and I turned my back on both of them. "There will be downstream implications of my reviving you, too. Oscar Knight will come after me harder. I wanted to build a life here, not be staring over my shoulder constantly. Is that what you want for me?"

Harold herded Liberty around to face me. She still looked haggard, but the gleam in her eyes told me she was recovering quickly. "No, that's not what I want for you. Because that was my life for years, and I didn't have friends to back me. I want you to have the life I didn't." She stepped around Harold and went to the espresso machine. "Renata, make me a coffee."

"Don't order my friends around," I said, as Ren got up to do Liberty's bidding. "And maybe they'll be your friends, too."

"I'm happy to make you a coffee, Miss Brighton," Ren said. "It's time to reclaim that smell."

"Thank you, Renata," the old woman said. "Please call me Liberty. And just so you know, I'll be protecting you girls, your stores and your dogs. While Oscar was busy living his life, I had time to mull over my magic, if not the energy to use it."

Ren served us all a steaming cup, and we toasted to the future of our stores and more. But then my phone rang.

"Don't answer it," Liberty said, retreating to stand in the kitchen doorway.

"We can't avoid it forever," I said, pressing the button to accept the video call. "Hey, Mom." I smiled at the two faces pressed to the screen. "Hey, Gran."

"Janelle Brighton," Mom said. "I've been calling and calling all evening. My mother's intuition has lit up the Briars. You've been into some serious magic, young lady."

"It's all fine," I said. "We're just sitting around the kitchen having a coffee with Cousin Liberty."

I let that bomb drop and watched their faces. There was skepticism, surprise and then, after I directed the phone's camera at Liberty, downright shock.

"Libby?" Gran said. "Is that really you?"

Liberty backed right out of the kitchen. "Don't involve me in your newfangled technology."

"Is that my dress?" Mom asked. "Were you rifling in my wardrobe, Cousin Liberty?"

She poked her head back in. "I came without suitcases, Shelley.

Obviously I needed something to wear. We need to hire a personal shopper for you."

Ren went back to huddle on her stool and Sinda joined her. Now it was a family affair.

"Can we hit a reset button and start over?" I propped the phone up on the counter. "This was a shock for me but probably even more so for you, Gran."

Bridie had never looked so nonplussed. "My cousin. I lost my cousin over thirty years ago. It broke my heart. You were closer to me than my own sister, Libby."

That was enough to bring Liberty back into the room. "It wasn't by choice, Bridie. And there wasn't a thing I could do to let you know. Oscar Knight and his cronies left me for dead in my own home and there was precious little left when Janelle found me."

"How?" Mom asked. "I went half a dozen times and didn't pick up a thing, Liberty."

Liberty smiled for the first time since the phone rang. "Harold's been keeping an eye on her since she got back. A herding dog is such a blessing."

"Ah," Mom said. "This ghost dog connection... I told Janelle it was unprecedented."

"Very much so," Liberty said. "I'm very grateful she picked up that gift. It's not strong in the Brightons, is it?"

Mom and Gran both pressed their lips together, clearly unwilling to speculate on the origins of that particular talent.

"How exactly did she resolve your predicament?" Mom asked. "That was a very powerful spell."

"Sometimes the solutions are deceptively simple," Liberty said. "Everyday magic."

Bixby cleared his voice conspicuously. "It did cost Janelle quite a bit, for all its simplicity."

I ran my hand over his sleek back. "I'm fine. Your tea really worked wonders, Mom."

Mom leaned into her phone till she was one fierce green eye. "Did you drain my child, Liberty?"

"Not by a long shot, Shelley. She's got a bottomless pit of energy. Regardless, I left her with a full tank, and more." She spun the phone around and met Mom's eye. "You'll see when you get home. When can we expect you?"

"We have a little situation here," Mom said. "Currently unresolved."

Gran took her turn leaning in. "Someone's trying to throw me under buses, Liberty. Or throw them at me."

Liberty flicked the phone away. "Oscar, I'm sure. For pity's sake, Bridie. If you'd just use the genes nature gave you this wouldn't be a problem."

"What genes?" I asked. "Gran doesn't have any magic. Like Aunt Eva and Jilly."

Liberty flounced across the kitchen, gesticulating. "Do you think nature makes mistakes like that? People choose." Coming back, she stared into the phone again. "Choose differently, Bridie, so your family doesn't need to come down there and protect you."

Gran sighed. "Janelle, can you take her back where you found her? Or at least let Oscar know where she is?"

I laughed. "I'm not throwing Liberty to Oscar Knight, Gran. But he's probably going to come after me for saving her. I hate to say it, Mom, but I need you to come home. Bring Gran with you."

"You can come to the opening," Ren called.

"Opening?" Mom said.

Liberty took the phone again. "Of Whimsy. Her store, Shelley. Get with the program. This means a lot to Janelle, and I, for one, intend to be there with bells on."

CHAPTER TWENTY-EIGHT

The bell over the door at Whimsy tinkled merrily and then burst into what could only be called a serenade when Liberty walked into my store a week later, on opening day.

"I'm so pleased Renata found my old doorbell," she said, striding across to the counter, and flinging her coat onto a chair. "I charmed that bell and now it's charming a new generation."

She was wearing a gorgeous brocade jacket over a matching dress. Her long hair was braided and twisted into a shining coronet and her makeup was impeccable. Tall heels gave her a good inch over my own tall heels. Since Liberty's return, I'd unpacked my own clothes. It was time to stop hiding under Mom's nerdy fashions. If Liberty could flaunt it, I would, too.

I walked over and flipped the sign on the door to open. Mom and Gran had declined to come home after yet another incident at the Briars, but Liberty was flying down later to get things sorted out.

"This is a big day, my friend," Ren said. "A huge day."

"The culmination of many years of dreaming," I said.

Liberty glanced around the store. "It's quaint, Janelle, but really... dream bigger."

"Don't insult my friends, Liberty," I said, deliberately dropping the "cousin." "I'm here because of them, and showcasing their wares, as well."

Sinda's designs sparkled from displays all over the store. Every piece of jewelry she had—with the notable exception of the ghost dog collection—lit up the shelves and tables. Time had run short for stocking products, so I'd arranged what I had nicely and filled in the gaps with Ren's baked goods and jars of colorful preserves. The effect was so pretty that the first group of women who came in gasped in delight.

"Really?" Liberty muttered. Her scorn was more for show, I knew, because her fingers toyed with the sheepdog brooch in her lapel that Sinda had given her earlier. Unlike the rest of us, Liberty preferred a pin to a pendant.

Bixby collapsed on his side on the counter. "Is this my life now? Ladies gasping over jewelry and preserves? I came back for this?"

Harold sent up a little breeze that blew my dog's ears back, and Bixby stared over the edge at him coldly.

"Stop it, bad boys," Bijou said. "No drama on Witchy's big day."

Liberty looked around the circle of dogs and smiled. If we had nothing else in common, we most certainly shared a love of all things canine and an ability to enjoy their chatter.

The bell over the door gave a strangled squeak and Liberty turned quickly. "Octavia? Is it really you?"

Another elegant woman, this one likely in her sixties with perfect blonde highlights, looked up with a smile. "Liberty! I heard you were back. Wherever have you been all these years?"

She came over with hands outstretched, and Harold quickly stepped between them.

While the new woman stared down at the dog with clear blue eyes, Cousin Liberty's mouth worked, likely struggling with an answer. Finally, she cleared her throat and said, "I was never away, Octavia. I was spelled into oblivion and ultimately trapped in my own home for decades. By your husband."

Mrs. Knight reared back and her manicured fingers clutched her pearls. "Pardon me? That cannot be true, Liberty. Oscar would never do such a thing."

"He would and he did, Tavi. And worse, he killed my dog." Liberty's voice got high and tense as she touched Harold's ears. "This dog—Harold—is the love of my life. And Oscar killed him."

Octavia's brow furrowed, and if she was faking her innocence, she was doing a very good job of it. "I don't understand, Liberty. Harold is obviously alive. My dear, are you feeling quite well?"

"She's fully recovered," I said, stepping forward to introduce myself and shake Octavia's hand. "What Cousin Liberty is saying is that Mr. Knight accosted her some time ago and then left Harold to die."

Mrs. Knight blinked rapidly. "Why on earth would he do such a thing? Oscar loves dogs. We have a ridgeback ourselves."

"I've met her," I said. "She's gorgeous. Perhaps this discussion is better left till another day. Welcome to Whimsy, Mrs. Knight. I've looked forward to meeting you."

"Do buy something," Liberty said. "It's the least the Knights can do for the Brightons, considering."

I started leading Liberty away. "Only if you see something you like, Mrs. Knight."

Octavia started grabbing things off the shelves, tossing an alpaca throw right on top of Bixby. "Hey," he barked. "Innocent bystander, here."

"Cousin Liberty," I said, in the back room, "Octavia was innocent. I touched her rings and got nothing but confusion."

"Confusion... or denial?" Liberty said. "She married the man."

"Just the same, let them sort it out between them." A musical trill over the door made me jump. "It's Drew Gillock."

Liberty's expression softened. "That bell never lies. He's sweet on you."

"If he still remembers," I said, glaring at her before I went back out. "Harold, keep her here, please."

"He obeys me," Liberty said.

"And me," I called back. "That's how this works."

The heap on the counter had grown and Mr. Bixby was now riding around under Sinda's arm as Octavia Knight continued to collect our stock. There would be nothing left at the rate she was going.

I walked over to meet Drew. He was standing by the window, examining a jar of strawberry jam with great interest. "Congratulations," he said. "Things seem to be flying off the shelves."

"And we haven't been open long. I hope it's a good sign. As Ren just said, this store is my dream come true."

He smiled, but there was a restrained quality to it. "I hope so, too. You'll need to be careful not to cross the wrong people. There seem to be some long-held grudges on Main Street."

"Some dating back to Cousin Liberty's day, apparently."

After staring briefly at Liberty, who was blocked in the back room by Harold, Drew met my eyes squarely. "If I'm not overreaching, Janelle, there's something I'd like to say."

"Overreaching?" I asked. Was his use of the word a coincidence?

"Yes, I believe that was your cousin Liberty's word. She used it twice, and it sounded like a warning."

"Uh-oh," Mr. Bixby said, as Sinda passed the dog into my arms. "That's an unexpected twist. What else does Big Red have up his uniform sleeve?"

"I'm—I'm surprised you remember that, Drew. There was such a commotion in the Skinner house that night."

"Now Liberty's house, I see. She found them a new one and helped them pack. The children seemed to know and like her."

"How interesting," I said. "I guess the house was imbued with her distinctive personality."

"They weren't as big on the dog," he added. "Everywhere he goes, wind seems to follow. He's a helicopter in canine form."

Harold had left Liberty and was stalking Drew. His belly was on the floor but his ears were forward, so I knew it was a game.

"My family is pretty quirky," I said. "Did I warn you about that?"

I shook my finger at the sheepdog and Harold dashed back to Liberty, tailless backside wriggling. The sheer joy of living hadn't left any of my rescues.

Finally Drew's smile seemed more genuine. "My family is quirky, too. Did I warn you about that?"

"Good one," Bixby said. "He's dishing it right back at you."

I tipped my head. "Maybe. I can't remember."

"There's an awful lot of forgetting going on around this town. I was mildly confused myself for a bit but these things pass quickly for me."

"Same for Ethan, and now Norm. They're next door making coffee for us. Ren's still afraid of the machine."

Drew turned the jar of jam in his hand and then continued. "It's hard to uphold the law in a town like this. Emergency personnel don't seem to recall what happened with Diggory Waring. His mind cleared long enough to make a partial confession about Mitzy, however. I hope it's legitimate."

Reaching for his arm, I said, "It is. I promise you."

He stepped away from my hand. The movement was subtle, and his smile softened the blow.

"Oooh boy, that's gotta sting, Janny," Mr. Bixby said. "Big Red's giving you the cold shoulder. Literally."

Drew moved away even more. "We'll talk about it later. Over dinner, perhaps?"

The tension seeped out of me so quickly I nearly dropped Bixby, eliciting a sharp yap of reproof. "Hey. Careful. At least until I get my wings."

"That would be great," I told Drew. My heart sang like the bell over the door. A date! We had a date!

"Ethan's invited all of us to the restaurant opening," he said, easing back to join another group of customers.

"Maybe not a date," Mr. Bixby said. "He's keeping you guessing. I underestimated Red. And he most definitely did not overreach."

"Janelle," Octavia called. "I'm ready to cash out."

I walked back to the counter with Bixby. "You really don't need to buy all this, Mrs. Knight. I hope you didn't feel obligated."

"Nonsense. I love giving budding entrepreneurs a helping hand." She fished her credit card out of her purse. "I'll have unique gifts for everyone this Christmas."

Ren had scanned and bagged most of the items and all I had to do was ring up the jewelry. Octavia had selected half a dozen of Sinda's creations.

"Pin this to my lapel, would you darling?" she asked. "I want my husband to see it right away."

It was a little gecko, with ruby eyes, and as I tried to pin it to her coat, it seemed to squirm beneath my fingertips.

Make that slither.

I very nearly stuck her with the pin when the bell over the door gave a familiar blast, and a wave of nausea passed over me.

"Step away from my wife," Oscar Knight called, gliding over with his usual serpentine grace.

"Oscar, relax," Mrs. Knight said. "She's pinning on a brooch, the most adorable lizard." Glancing down, she touched it. "From this angle, it looks like a snake."

"From any angle it looks like a snake," Bixby said. "They're unmistakable, really."

I finished with the brooch and straightened. "Hello, Oscar. Welcome to my grand opening. Your wife has supported me beyond my wildest hopes."

He looked somewhat mollified. "She's like that, my Tavi. Everyone loves her."

I patted the pin and moved away. "Mrs. Knight, Oscar and I are on the town's Christmas planning committee together."

"Please call me Tavi," she said. "If what Liberty said is true, my family owes yours a rather significant apology."

Oscar's eyes darted around the store and landed on Liberty, who stood with her shoulders back and her chin up. Her green eyes sent a flare of warning. "Hello, Oscar. You look well."

His shoulders went back, too. "As do you, Liberty."

"Surprisingly, I am. I had a chance to brief Tavi on what happened."

Octavia put her hand on her husband's sleeve. "Please tell me you didn't leave Liberty to die, Oscar. And Harold, her dog." Her eyelids fluttered. "We're a dog family."

Oscar swallowed hard before speaking. "Tavi, you've been misinformed. I did have words with the senior Miss Brighton. When she left unexpectedly, I searched for her dog, to no avail. He looked very much like this one."

"Very much," Liberty said. "I've been lucky with my Aussies. Handsome and loyal."

"We really must be going," Oscar said. "The car's right out front, Tavi. I'll grab the bags."

Mrs. Knight squeezed my arm. "Come to dinner, darling. I know you were good friends with my Jared."

This time, I was the one swallowing hard. "Oh yes, Mrs. Knight. I think about him often."

She gave me a sly wink. "He's still single, you know. Hasn't met the right girl."

"There's an idea," Bixby said as Octavia walked out of the store. "Keep your friends close and your enemies closer."

"If you so much as think about dating that boy, I'll spell you till your head spins, Janelle," Liberty said, coming out of the back room.

"I like your wife, Oscar. Everyone does. How you've duped her this long is beyond comprehension."

He gathered the bags quickly and turned from Liberty to me. "Never come between a man and his wife, Janelle. There's precious little room."

"Never come between a Brighton and her dog, Oscar," Liberty said. "Word to the wise."

Harold responded to my signal to herd her away, but her grumbles were audible.

"We're going to have our hands full," Bixby said, nipping at Oscar's sleeve as he collected the last bag.

Oscar glowered at me as he adjusted the many bags. "This won't end well, I'm afraid. There's a lot more I could say about Liberty, you know."

"But your wife is waiting," I said. "And I just want to enjoy this wonderful day."

He backed away. "I'll visit again soon."

"We'll find just the right Christmas gift for your wife," I said. "A one-of-a-kind design."

His mouth opened but whatever snarky comment he made got lost in a sneeze as Harold circled him. Oscar tried to lift his sleeve in time to block it and dropped half the bags.

"I'll get those for you, Mr. Knight," Drew said, leaving the other customers and coming forward.

"Don't touch them." Oscar sneezed again as the whirling dog got faster. "Get my man."

Glancing out the window, I saw his slick henchman was already coming to the door. I'd never seen the guy move so fast. He gathered all the bags so that Oscar was able to stride away unencumbered.

Drew followed the two men out and didn't look back.

At first I was disappointed, but looking around, joy quickly filled my heart again. I was here. Home. Surrounded by friends and dogs in my beloved store.

"I'll leave you kids to enjoy." Liberty slipped her arms into a fur coat that I told myself was a good fake. "Harold and I have things to do."

She hugged me for the first time and while she didn't say it, I knew she was proud of me. So proud I almost didn't mind the fur.

Mr. Bixby pretended to rub away a tear. "Family. It's enough to make you cry."

After seeing Liberty out, I circulated among my customers until there was nothing left on my shelves.

Then I turned the sign to closed fully an hour early.

Ren shut the blinds and I spun around and around with Bixby, while she did pirouettes with Bijou, the circus dog. Sinda settled for popping the cork on a bottle of champagne.

"Enough?" I asked, setting Bixby on the counter and accepting a flute of bubbly.

"Enough to make me heave, if that's what you're after," the dog said. "I'm already overtaxed from the magical flatulence."

I planted a kiss on his sleek head. "We're celebrating a new era. Don't suppose you'd like a sip?"

"Newsflash, Miss Brighton," he said. "Dachshunds don't drink and they don't dance, either."

I laughed. "Luckily they do nearly everything else better than everyone else."

Mr. Bixby rolled onto his back to show off his tan belly freckles. "I'll drink to that."

When Cousin Liberty is framed for murder, Janelle is on the hook to solve the mystery before Christmas in Wyldwood Springs.

Luckily, she finds a couple of unexpected allies, one of whom happens to be handsome, hairy and haunting a local store. Don't miss **I ONLY HAUNT TO BE WITH YOU**.

Would you like to try my other two lighthearted—but non-magical—mystery series for dog lovers? If so, I invite you to join my newsletter group at **ellenriggs.com/mystic-mutts-opt-in**. You can try the "Bought the Farm" series for free and hear all about my adorable dogs. Hope to see you there!

More Books by Ellen Riggs

Mystic Mutt Mysteries Paranormal Cozy

- I Want You to Haunt Me
- You Can't Always Get What You Haunt
- Any Way You Haunt It
- I Only Haunt to be with You

- All I Haunt Is You
- Do You Haunt to Know a Secret?
- All I Haunt for Christmas

Bought-the-Farm Cozy Mystery Series

- A Dog with Two Tales (*prequel*)
- Dogcatcher in the Rye
- Dark Side of the Moo
- A Streak of Bad Cluck
- Till the Cat Lady Sings
- Alpaca Lies
- Twas the Bite Before Christmas
- Swine and Punishment
- The Cat and the Riddle
- Don't Rock the Goat
- Swan with the Wind
- How to Get a Neigh with Murder
- Tweet Revenge
- For Love Or Bunny
- Between a Squawk and a Hard Place
- Double Dog Dare
- Deerly Departed
- Think Outside the FoxMouse of Ill Repute
- Bee All and End All
- Sheep with One Eye Open
- Roo the Day

Bought-the-Farm Mysteries - Boxed Sets

- Bought the Farm Mysteries - Books 1-3
- Bought the Farm Mysteries - Books 4-6
- Bought the Farm Mysteries - Books 7-9

- Bought the Farm Mysteries - Books 10-12
- Bought the Farm Mysteries - Books 13-15
- Bought the Farm Mysteries - Books 1-10

Books by Ellen Riggs and Sandy Rideout

Dog Town Series

- Ready or Not in Dog Town (The Beginning)
- Bitter and Sweet in Dog Town (Labor Day)
- A Match Made in Dog Town (Thanksgiving)
- Lost and Found in Dog Town (Christmas)
- Calm and Bright in Dog Town (Christmas)
- Tried and True in Dog Town (New Year's)
- Yours and Mine in Dog Town (Valentine's Day)
- Nine Lives in Dog Town (Easter)
- Great and Small in Dog Town (Memorial Day)
- Bold and Blue in Dog Town (Independence Day)
- Better or Worse in Dog Town (Labor Day)

Dog Town Boxed Sets

- Mischief in Dog Town - Books 1-3
- Mischief in Dog Town - Books 4-7
- Mischief in Dog Town - Books 8-10
- Mischief in Dog Town - The Complete Series

Made in the USA
Las Vegas, NV
14 September 2024

95253994R00125